# THEO SLUGG
## in low spirits

Then a movement caught Theo's eye. It was Mrs Jellicon's handkerchief, which she held in her right hand, and it stood out clearly in the darkness. She shook it casually but Theo could see that actually she was signalling to a man standing behind her.

Theo stared. The man was a ghost. There was no doubt about it; the same bluish glow that Grandma and the other ghosts all had was clearly visible in the darkness. He was smartly dressed in a long tailcoat but he looked like a thug. Theo shivered. He didn't like the look of this.

Other titles by Simon Goswell:

# Theo Slugg in Dead Trouble

# THEO slugg

## in low spirits

**Simon Goswell**

■SCHOLASTIC

Scholastic Children's Books,
Commonwealth House, 1–19 New Oxford Street,
London, WCIA INU, UK
A division of Scholastic Ltd
London ~ New York ~ Toronto ~ Sydney ~ Auckland
Mexico City ~ New Delhi ~ Hong Kong

First published in the UK by Scholastic Ltd, 2004

Copyright © Simon Goswell, 2004

ISBN 0 439 97766 5

All rights reserved

Printed and bound by Nørhaven Paperback A/S, Denmark

10 9 8 7 6 5 4 3 2 1

The right of Simon Goswell to be identified as the author of this work has been asserted
by him in accordance with the Copyright, Designs and Patents Act, 1988.

# A NOTE OF CAUTION

It is quite possible that you have never heard a ghost. But have you considered that you might have heard one without realizing it? Have you ever thought that you could hear somebody call your name and then found that there was no one there? Yes? Well, then you know what I'm talking about.

If you hear a ghost, don't get alarmed. It doesn't always mean that trouble is on the way. Only sometimes.

But just in case something terrible is about to happen, it's as well to be on your guard. Then you can run for it if things start looking grim. After all, where ghosts are concerned, there's no telling where the trouble will lead to. . .

Theo looked around nervously. After a day at the beach, he and his family had stopped at Luigi's Café on the way home. Theo really liked Luigi's. It was one of his favourite places. The only trouble was that ever since his dead grandma had spoken to him from the mirror, he was always slightly anxious when he was there. He couldn't help half expecting her to leap out at him. Either her or that strange not-really-dead girl, Alix. But today the café was quite busy. Perhaps they wouldn't turn up. Perhaps he could relax.

It was certainly a big relief that at last his sisters were quiet, their mouths full of food. Why did they have to sing, wherever they went? They'd sung songs at the beach and so many people had stopped to listen it had turned into quite a performance. What an embarrassment! Theo had spent most of the day digging a large hole in the sand so that he could hide.

"You had a nice day at the beach, my friends?" said Nigel.

Nigel ran the café. He spoke with an Italian accent but he came from Essex.

"Mmm," said Theo, slurping his milkshake.

"Yes, thank you, Nigel," said Mrs Slugg.

"The sea was cold!" said Kate, the eldest of Theo's fourteen sisters.

"It always is," said Theo.

"Which beach did you go to?" asked Nigel.

"The one below the tower," said Louise, Kate's twin.

"Ah, the Cringle's Tower," said Nigel.

"Yes, that crumbling old wreck," said Theo.

"A shame that they are going to knock it down, is it not?" said Nigel.

"Are they?" said Mrs Slugg. "I hadn't heard that."

"Yes, they were talking about it at work," said Mr Slugg. "Apparently Mr Jellicon is going to build a golf course with a clubhouse and restaurant where the tower is."

"Yes, I heard that," agreed Nigel, nodding sadly.

Cringle's Tower was an old building on the cliff top

above Bunting. It was supposed to have been built as a lookout tower. The story was that Captain Cringle had built it for his wife, so that she could watch for his ship returning from a long voyage.

"Oh, it'll be a shame if it's knocked down," said Mrs Slugg. "It's been there for ages – it's quite a landmark."

"It'll have to be passed by the planning committee," said Mr Slugg. "I expect there'll be something in the local paper. But I shouldn't think many people will object. It's a dilapidated old building."

"So it's falling down anyway," said Theo. "And it won't make any difference."

"But it's on all the postcards of Bunting," said Mrs Slugg. "The coaches stop there for the view."

"They haven't for a while," answered Mr Slugg. "It's been fenced off with barbed wire. The tower's overgrown with creepers and is a dangerously unstable structure. I expect there's a risk of falling masonry."

"Then it should be knocked down straight away," said Theo. "Someone might get hurt."

"No, they should rebuild it," said Louise. "It's a nice tower."

"I agree, my young friend," said Nigel. "It will be a great loss if it is knocked down. But, ah well, that is progress."

"Nigel," called a woman from behind the counter. "We need some more pancakes."

"All right, one moment," answered Nigel.

"Isn't that the woman from the library?" said Kate. "The one who's always finding music books for us."

"Ah yes," said Nigel, smiling. "Miss Sheldon. She helps me here on busy Sundays. Enjoy your meal, my friends." And he went off to make pancakes.

As they walked home, Theo's sisters sang more of their favourite songs. Theo walked a few steps behind everyone else so that he wasn't too close. He could hardly wait to get home to the peace and quiet of his corner of the lift. (It was to get away from his sisters' singing that he'd moved his bed into the lift in the first place.)

But as they approached Vanilla Villas he heard an even worse noise – wailing – and it was coming from the entrance hall. Nobody else seemed to hear it. Theo knew that that sort of wailing, the sort that only he could hear, was really bad news.

"Woe! Woe! Woe!"

Theo saw the woman as soon as he walked in through the front door. She was walking up and down the entrance hall, waving her hands in the air and wailing. She wore a long, old-fashioned dress of a dusty blue colour, her hair, powdered white, was done up on top of her head and over one eye was a black patch. But the telltale sign was the hazy blue glow around her. It was only slight but enough to confirm Theo's suspicions: she was a ghost.

Theo's heart sank. The last time he'd got involved with ghosts he'd ended up in no end of trouble. It had been his grandma's doing – his *three months' dead* grandma – who despite being dead and buried had come back to get some things done. She'd always been a person who'd done things and she wasn't going to let a little thing like being dead stop her. What's wrong with that, you might say? Well, nothing, except she insisted Theo help her. And Theo, who had never liked his bossy, rude grandma, was understandably not keen on that idea at all.

Now it seemed to be starting again. This must be Grandma's doing, thought Theo as the ghostly woman went on wailing. She came right up to Theo, waving her hands at him, her one eye staring wildly.

"Woe! Woe! Wooooe!"

Theo tried to ignore her. If he pretended that he couldn't see her then perhaps she'd give up and go away. His parents and his sisters were waiting for the lift to arrive, oblivious to the howling ghost beside them.

"The lift's a long time coming," said Mr Slugg.

"Woe!" wailed the woman. She walked right up to Theo, who was standing a little behind his sisters, and wailed in his left ear. He stared straight ahead.

"Perhaps somebody propped the door open," said Mrs Slugg.

"Woe! Woe!" wailed the woman in Theo's right ear. He looked at his shoes.

"We're going up the stairs," said Kate and Louise, the eldest twins. They set off up the steps.

"Woe! Woe! Woe!" wailed the woman, standing directly in front of Theo.

"I'll come too," said Mr Slugg. "I'll see what's wrong with the lift." He followed his daughters.

"Woe! Woe!"

As they waited for the lift to arrive, Florence and Beatrice, three years old, started singing:

*"The days of gloom are over, over, over!*
*Joy is here to stay."*

"Woe! Woe! Wooooe!" wailed the woman, two inches from Theo's face, and staring at him with her one, slightly bloodshot eye.

*"The villain's gone for ever, ever, ever!*
*Far, far away."*

"Woe! Woe! Woe!" wailed the woman, one inch from Theo's face.

*"Now everybody's happy. . ."*

"Woe!"

*". . .happy. . ."*

"Woe!"

*". . .hap—"*

"Oh, be quiet!" shouted Theo before he could stop himself.

Florence and Beatrice stopped singing immediately. Both let out a shriek and burst into tears.

"Theo! What are you thinking of? That's no way to behave," exclaimed Mrs Slugg. "It's all right, darlings." She comforted her daughters.

"Oh sorry, Mum. I didn't mean. . . It was just. . ." Theo gave up. He couldn't possibly explain.

"Woe! Woe! Woe!" wailed the woman. She waved her hands about in the air above her head and looked at the ceiling.

Theo bit his lip.

There was a "ping" as the lift arrived and the doors opened.

"I think you should wait there," said Mrs Slugg, ushering her daughters inside. "Then you'll have your room to yourself and be able to calm down before supper."

Theo nodded glumly. The lift doors closed and he was left alone with the wailing woman.

"Woe!" went on the woman, who had wandered off across the floor towards the janitor's room. The door opened and out came the janitor, Mr Windrush, carrying a dustpan and brush. Mr Windrush always carried a dustpan and brush. He liked collecting dust. He collected dust like you or I might collect stamps or coins. The shelves of his room were stacked high with jars full of the stuff, all carefully labelled.

For a moment, Theo hoped that Mr Windrush would say something and the ghost would stop wailing, but he just gave Theo a slight wave with his brush and disappeared back into his room.

There was a "ping" as the lift arrived back again. Theo rushed in and quickly pressed the button. But as the doors closed the woman's ghost appeared beside him.

"Woe!"

As the lift started going up, to Theo's intense relief the woman's ghost stayed at ground level. She stopped wailing and looked a bit surprised. Lifts seemed to be something new to her. The lift went up and she gradually disappeared through the floor. Her head and her waving arms remained for a second or two and then she was gone.

Theo sank on to his bed.

"Oh, no!" he groaned softly, holding his head in his hands.

He knew that wasn't the end of it. If his grandma was involved – and he was almost sure that she was – then there was bound to be more to come.

"Theo, don't just stand there, take these and put them on the table."

Theo jumped at the sound of his mother's voice. He'd been standing idly in the kitchen, lost in thought. Hurriedly he took the tray of soup bowls and carried it through to the dining room.

Mealtimes in the Slugg household were cramped affairs. There was only just enough room for everybody to sit down. Theo and his sisters squeezed around the two small dining tables. Mr and Mrs Slugg sat at a little camping table put up just for meals.

Theo put down his tray and put the bowls of soup on the place mats. He and his sisters all helped at mealtimes; laying the tables, carrying the plates of food to and from the kitchen and washing up afterwards. As soon as everything was ready, everybody sat down and the meal began.

Table manners are one of those things that help the world turn smoothly. It would go round quite well without them, but personally I'd rather share my dinner with people who are well-behaved than otherwise.

I'm not talking about snobbish stuff like on which side of your plate the pudding spoon should go or whether the turbot should be served with its head towards you or not. Just the basic stuff like you don't blow your nose on the tablecloth or eat with your mouth open.

"Is there beetroot in this?" asked Theo, looking suspiciously at his soup. His mother was still experimenting with Russian cuisine.

"No, Theo. It's minestrone," answered Mrs Slugg.

"That's Italian, isn't it, Mum?" said Clare.

"That's right."

"Maybe you can have Russian minestrone," suggested Theo.

"I doubt it," said Mr Slugg. "It wouldn't be minestrone, then, would it?"

"We're going to Russia, aren't we, Mum?" said Ruth.

"Well, I hope so, dear," said Mrs Slugg, who was hoping to take her daughters singing in Russia.

"I hope so, too," said Theo. "Then it will be lovely and quiet here."

"That's not a very nice thing to say," said Mrs Slugg.

"But —" protested Theo.

"All right, Theo," said Mr Slugg. "Eat your soup."

Theo fell silent, brooding. He wasn't generally nasty to his sisters. He'd moved his bed into the lift to keep out of their way but only because he didn't like their singing. Otherwise most of the time they got on all right. He was even quite proud of their singing success, although he didn't let on. But the wailing woman had made him edgy. If he was right and his grandma was up to something then he'd soon have her to deal with and he wasn't looking forward to that at all.

"Hey, I've remembered something!" cried Ruth.

"What, dear?" said Mrs Slugg.

"About the tower," said Ruth.

"What, Cringle's Tower?" asked Kate. "What about it?"

"Yes," said Ruth. "Something George Tetley said."

"What?" asked Lizzie, Jane and Penny, together.

**17**

"Well, George Tetley said it's haunted," said Ruth.

"I expect he was only trying to scare you, darling," said Mrs Slugg.

"I've heard that too," said Clare. "The ghost is a woman in a blue dress."

"That's right!" cried Ruth. "And guess what?"

"What?" asked Lizzie, Jane and Penny, together.

"She's only got one eye!" shrieked Ruth in delight.

At which point Theo choked in surprise and sprayed minestrone soup across the table.

Theo had to do double-duty with the washing up.

"What's got into you?" asked Theo's mother, as she stacked the dirty bowls by the sink. "You don't usually behave like this. Fancy spitting soup all over the table!"

"Sorry, Mum," mumbled Theo. "It was an accident, honestly." He could hardly say that he was upset because a ghost was haunting him. He didn't think his mother would have believed him. Annoyed that Grandma and her dead friends had got him into trouble once again, he got on with washing the seventeen soup bowls.

When he went to bed that evening, Theo didn't bother trying to sleep. He knew that sooner or later he'd be visited by the ghost of the one-eyed woman in the blue dress, and probably his grandma as well.

If, as he suspected, the ghost of the woman was in some way connected with Cringle's Tower, then that would explain her visits. His grandma was obviously planning something. That those plans would involve Theo, he wasn't in any doubt.

Theo stared moodily at the ceiling. He wasn't remotely keen on helping in any scheme of his grandma's, but his dad had mentioned that Mr Jellicon intended to demolish the tower and the fact that Jellicon was involved made Theo even less enthusiastic. The last time Theo had tangled with Josiah Jellicon it had not been a pleasant experience, and he had no wish to repeat it.

Theo waited. He played one of his video games to pass the time. But as the hours ticked by, and there was still no sign of either the woman or his grandma, he began to think that perhaps they weren't coming after all. He was getting sleepier and sleepier and although he did his best to stay awake, his eyelids drooped and he kept dozing off. At last he decided that the ghosts weren't coming. He got under the duvet and in a few seconds was fast asleep.

Five minutes later he was woken by wailing.

"Woe! Woe! Woooooe!"

"Urgghhhh!" groaned Theo.

It was the woman in the blue dress. There was no sign of Grandma. The woman hovered about the lift, waving her hands in the air like a windmill and wailing at the ceiling.

"Woe! Wooooe! Woe!"

"What? Tell me! What?" cried Theo, hoping the woman would talk sense. "Is it about that building? What's it called . . . Cringle's Tower?"

At the mention of the tower, the woman screeched, waved her hands at double the speed and wailed very loudly. "WOE! WOE! WOOOOOOE!"

This was too much for Theo.

"*OH, SHUT UP AND GO AWAY!*" he shouted in exasperation.

To Theo's surprise the woman instantly stopped wailing. She looked at Theo, her good eye brimming with tears and her lower lip trembling. Then she turned around and promptly disappeared through the wall of the lift, sobbing loudly.

"*Oh, buckets!*" muttered Theo. Now there'd be trouble.

Sure enough, about half an hour later the woman reappeared, this time with Grandma.

"Sit up, you horrid little worm," said Grandma, giving Theo a rough prod with her walking stick.

Theo sat up quickly and smiled as sweetly as he could. "Hello Grandma, how lovely to see you! I hope you're keeping well?" he chirped, not meaning a word of it.

"Don't you give me any of that *lovely to see you* rubbish!" said Grandma. "Do you think I was born yesterday? You're a rude and nasty little boy and you've just been very rude and very nasty to a friend of mine. You had better apologize straight away or I'll see that you regret it."

Theo's Grandma was not given to making idle threats. If she said she would do something then she generally did it. Only something on the scale of a very large earthquake would be sufficient to stop her. Theo, who wasn't like even a very small earthquake, hadn't a hope.

"I'm very sorry, Grandma. I didn't mean –"

Grandma scowled. "Hmm. I don't believe it. Anyway, you can say sorry properly to Mrs Cringle. Ethel, come here. Theo is going to apologize to you."

The woman in the blue dress had been standing limply at the back of the lift. She floated nervously forward.

"I'm very sorry I upset you, Mrs Cringle," said Theo.

The woman, glancing anxiously at Grandma, nodded and compressed her lips into a thin smile.

"That's better," said Grandma. "Now then—"

"Don't tell me," said Theo. "Let me guess – she's my second cousin nine times removed?"

"Don't interrupt, you slimy little stickleback. She's not one of your relations at all," said Grandma. "I told you – except you weren't listening – she's a friend of mine. If you did less talking and more listening you might learn something."

Theo was relieved to hear that Ethel Cringle was not one of his relations. Theo's grandma had introduced him to a good many of his dead relatives and they all seemed to be utterly hopeless. Theo thought that if someone was giving away prizes for hopelessness Mrs Cringle would win them all.

"As I was about to say, before I was so rudely interrupted," went on Grandma, "Mrs Cringle's husband, Captain William Cringle, built a tower—"

No sooner had Grandma said the word "tower" than Mrs Cringle let out a shriek like an owl might make if it was a very upset owl indeed. She started up again with her wailing-and-waving-hands routine.

"Woe! Wooooe!"

"*Oh Ethel, do SHUT UP!*" bellowed Grandma.

Theo failed to suppress a snigger. Grandma shot him a look that would have turned most warm-blooded creatures to stone. Mrs Cringle fell silent. She slumped on to the floor and sat there, looking as if she'd just been stunned by a large blunt object.

"Now then, Theo," continued Grandma, "you won't know this because you never read the news-papers, but Jellicon is planning to knock down the . . . umm . . . you know. . ."

"Tall building on the cliff top?" suggested Theo, realizing that his grandma was avoiding using the word "tower" so as not to start Mrs Cringle off on another lot of wailing.

"Yes, that's it," said Grandma, looking sideways at Mrs Cringle. "Well, he's going to knock it down and build a golf club or something. Anyway, the point is that he must be stopped. And that's where you come in."

"Oh no, it isn't," said Theo.

"Don't be ridiculous," said Grandma. "This is important. Alix will help and you will too."

"I'm not helping," said Theo, and he doubted if Alix

**24**

would either. It was one of the things he really liked about the not-really-dead girl; she stood up to his grandma. "If Jellicon's involved, I'm having nothing to do with it."

"But all you've got to do is go to the planning meeting and—"

"I won't and that's that," said Theo stubbornly. "Anyway, who cares about a rotten old tow— . . . *tall building* that's falling down anyway?"

"I'll have you know that it's a very important haunt for Mrs Cringle. And not only that but it's where the annual Hallowe'en party is held."

"Why should I help?" said Theo. "She's not a dead relative this time, Grandma. And a party venue for a lot of dead people? Find somewhere else!"

"But the party's always been held there. It's a tradition going back at least two hundred years! We can't just find somewhere else."

"I'm not interested and I don't care," said Theo. He was determined to resist his grandma.

"Theo Slugg, you're a disappointment. I thought that you might be becoming more caring and considerate but I see you are still the selfish little toad that you always were."

"Why should I help you? Look what happened the

last time – I got trapped in Jellicon's factory, almost arrested, locked in a cupboard AND I nearly ended up in a vat of Jellicon's jam. Help? With Jellicon involved? Give me one reason why I should!"

"Because I'm your grandmother."

"Grandma, you're dead! I've my own life to lead."

"So you don't care about your family?"

"Argh! Always family!" groaned Theo. "I've enough family already! Ask somebody else! Ask one of my sisters if family is so important!"

"Silly little twerp. What do you take me for? You know perfectly well your sisters would be no help. I don't need a load of soppy songs."

Theo was slightly cheered by his grandma's words. But he wasn't going to budge. "Go away, Grandma. I'm not going to help with your plans. The last time just got me into trouble. I don't care what you say, I won't do it."

Grandma stood looking at Theo, her face like thunder. Theo waited for her to speak. He knew exactly what she was going to say. He saw the words coming as if they were an express train. And after she'd said them Theo knew that all hell would break loose until she got her way.

"Hmm, so that's your answer, is it?" said Grandma,

thumping her stick on the floor. "Well, we'll see about that!" She turned, and dragging the whimpering Mrs Cringle with her, stomped off. "Mark my words, Theo Slugg, we'll see about that!"

If you are one of those people who enjoys television, you'll know that there can be nothing more annoying than when the thing goes wrong. It can ruin your day and the chances are you'll be in a very bad mood until it's fixed and working again.

If you're not one of those people, then of course you won't understand this at all. You'll quite likely wonder what all the fuss is about and go back to your trombone or your scale model of HMS *Indefatigable* or whatever it is you do in your spare time.

When Theo woke up next morning and switched on his television to play his favourite video game, to his dismay, there wasn't the picture he expected on the screen. Instead of the control room of the Starship *Explorer* there were a lot of little black birds on a pink background. The birds squawked and danced around the screen. Nothing Theo tried would get rid of them. All the games and television channels had the same result: a screen full of dancing little black birds.

"Argh!" cried Theo in frustration. "What's wrong with the thing?"

At that moment the lift started travelling downwards. Somebody must have pressed the button on a lower floor to call the lift. It stopped at the ground floor and Theo peeped round his curtain to see who got in. He was pleased to see it was the janitor, Mr Windrush.

"Hello there," said Mr Windrush, who pushed a large box of cleaning things into the lift and then pressed the button for the basement. "All right?"

"No," said Theo.

"Oh," said Mr Windrush. "What's the matter?"

"My television's gone wrong," said Theo. "Look!"

Mr Windrush peered at the television through his large black-rimmed spectacles. He knew a bit about televisions and had helped with the aerial when Theo had first moved into the lift. He pressed a few buttons. The crows continued to dance about the screen.

"It's dimensional interference," he said at last. "It should clear itself eventually."

Theo hadn't any idea what he was talking about.

"Ah, there we are," said Mr Windrush.

Theo looked at the screen. The Starship *Explorer* was back again. The little black birds had disappeared.

"Brilliant!" cried Theo. "Thank you, Mr Windrush."

But the moment Mr Windrush got out at the basement the black birds came back again.

Theo tried fiddling with the knobs but it was no good.

Feeling miserable, Theo pressed the lift button and started putting on his clothes. When the lift reached the third floor, he got out and let himself into his family's flat. Perhaps after breakfast it would be all right.

But it wasn't. The little black birds were still there.

With nothing else to do, Theo thought that he'd work on a school project that he had to finish before the start of term. He hunted among his things until he found the folder. The project was called "Aluminium – A World Resource" and Theo had so far written four words. Theo looked at them:

*Aluminium is a metal.*

Well, it was a start. What should he write next?

Theo hadn't any idea.

He turned his television back on just in case the birds had gone.

They hadn't.

With a big sigh, Theo picked up his project folder and let himself back into the flat. He'd see if he could find some information on the Internet. Fortunately, his sisters had gone out for a singing lesson so the computer was free. Theo switched it on.

The welcome screen flickered briefly and then the background changed to pink. Theo watched in alarm as a line of little black birds appeared. They started dancing and squawking.

"That's fun!" said Theo's mother, looking over his shoulder.

"Hmm. I can't get rid of it," muttered Theo.

"I hope it's not a virus," said his mother.

"I don't think it is. . ." said Theo. He had an idea of where the little black birds might have come from. He had a suspicion that a certain ghostly grandma might have something to do with it. If he was right, then it seemed likely that the birds wouldn't disappear until he'd agreed to help Grandma with her latest scheme.

The last time it had been singing toads. This time it was dancing birds. You might think that this wasn't much to be bothered about, though Theo had a distinct feeling that he was being backed into a corner.

He wasn't going to give in that easily. It would be hard but he was up to the challenge. He was determined.

Theo gritted his teeth.

There was certainly worse to come.

As his television and the computer were useless, Theo decided that he'd go to the public library. He thought he'd try and do some more to his project there. There were computers in the library so he would be able to search the Internet and there was sure to be a book with some information too.

Theo was feeling pretty fed up. The school work had to be done some time but it wasn't his idea of fun. He'd rather be at home playing video games. And to make matters worse, it was raining. He didn't like getting wet.

At the library, Theo stopped to look at the videos which were displayed just inside the door. He'd been waiting for the film *Total Disaster* and to his delight he saw that it was in. Then he realized there was probably no point in borrowing it. His television would just show a lot of little black birds. He was just putting it back when someone tapped his elbow.

"Hello Mr Theo, my friend."

Theo turned round. It was Nigel, the man who ran Luigi's Café. He was carrying a huge stack of books.

"Nigel!" cried Theo. "I didn't know you read books."

"Oh yes," said Nigel, smiling. "I have recently dis-covered the reading of books. It is a great pleasure, is it not?"

"Er . . . yes, Nigel," agreed Theo.

"Well, I must be getting on," said Nigel. "I see you, my friend."

Theo sat down at a computer, keyed in his name and library number and waited while the computer checked his details. The library logo appeared briefly and then the screen went "pop" and changed to pink. On came the dancing black birds. Theo stared at the screen open-mouthed.

But then the birds did something different. They arranged themselves in a rectangle, like a picture frame. The pink space in the middle changed to white and as Theo watched a photograph of his grandma appeared. All the birds clapped their wings. Grandma was grinning.

Theo didn't wait to see any more. He switched off the computer in disgust. How had his grandma done it? He'd no idea. So that was that. Never mind, he'd make do with a book instead. He went to look at the bookshelves.

After searching the shelves for some time Theo finally found what he was looking for. It was called *A Brief Introduction to the Aluminium Industry*. It was a big book and it seemed to be stuck at the back of the shelf. Theo gave it a tug. The shelf wobbled slightly but the book didn't budge. Theo tugged a bit harder. The shelf wobbled a bit more and Theo watched in horror as all the other books slid forwards. They started to fall off the shelf, one after another, each making a loud "thump" as it hit the floor. Soon all the books, except the one that Theo wanted, were lying in a heap on the floor.

Theo mouthed "Sorry" at the librarian. It was Miss Sheldon, who had been at Luigi's Café on Sunday. Theo picked up the books and was just putting them back when he saw what looked like a severed head on the shelf in front of him. Theo dropped the books with a crash.

"Wat! I wish you wouldn't surprise me like that!" cried Theo.

The ghost of Wat Kemp, Theo's Grandma's second apprentice torturer, wearing his greasy cap and apron, stepped away from the shelves. "I only meant it as a joke," mumbled Wat.

"You gave me quite a shock," said Theo.

"Could you please be a bit quieter?" said the librarian, who had come over to where Theo was still trying to put the books back. "This is supposed to be a place for peaceful study."

"I'm sorry," began Theo. "The books, they. . ."

"Yes, all right. Leave them there. I'll put them back," said the librarian. "Is this the one you wanted? There's a desk over there if you want to look at it."

Theo took the big book on aluminium over to the desk and sat down. The desk was in a corner and luckily there was no one else nearby. Wat followed, grinning.

"Won't you please help over the tower?" whispered Wat.

Theo looked at Wat. Of all his dead relatives he liked Wat the most. He hated to disappoint him but he really couldn't face battling with Jellicon again. He didn't think he stood a chance this time.

"I'm sorry, Wat. I don't want to get involved,"

whispered Theo. He kept an eye on the librarian who had sat down again.

"Oh go on!" pleaded Wat. "It's not Mrs Cringle. She's as batty as a bodkin. But the party. It's always been held there – it's a tradition."

Theo shook his head. Then an idea occurred to him.

"But won't there still be a ghost tower, even after the real tower has been knocked down? Can't you use that?"

"Buildings don't always become ghosts. And it's not the same," said Wat, sadly. "Not for Hallowe'en. It's not real haunting. It has to be haunting for Hallowe'en."

"Too bad, Wat," said Theo. "There's nothing I can do."

"Alix could help," suggested Wat.

"No, Wat."

Wat wandered away but after a minute or two he came back to where Theo was sitting.

"I nearly forgot," he said. "I meant to tell you that your grandfather told me—"

"You know my grandfather?" exclaimed Theo. His grandfather had died before he was born. Theo had looked at the family photos, wondering what he'd been like. His mum had told him that he'd been a librarian and that he'd thought that books held the answer to practically everything. "Knowledge is power" had been his motto.

"Yes," said Wat. "He's learning me to read and write. Well, he told me that there's a book on it."

"On what, Wat?"

"On Captain Cringle's tower. It was for everybody, your grandfather said, not just Mrs Cringle. That's why the party's held there. It's all in the book."

"Where is this book?" asked Theo.

"In the library, of course," said Wat, looking at Theo as if he was stupid.

Wat started searching his pockets. He emptied them on to the desk. There was a bit of string, an apple core, a bit of chain and what looked like an ancient pair of handcuffs. "Here," said Wat, who'd found what he was looking for. He put a crumpled bit of paper on the desk.

It was a bit of ghost paper, very thin and almost transparent. Theo peered at the writing. It was hardly visible.

"My name is MAT," read Theo, aloud.

"Oh!" said Wat, grinning sheepishly. "I get my letters muddled." He turned over the bit of paper.

"*The Cringle Bequest* by the Reverend Algernon Brusset," read Theo. This writing was different, very neat and tidy. "So that's about the tower?"

Wat shrugged. "But you'll read it?" he asked, hopefully.

Theo thought for a moment. He was tempted. The thought that his grandfather had suggested the book attracted him. But then he remembered Jellicon. He shook his head. "Sorry, Wat. I don't want to get involved."

"Not even a little?" asked Wat.

"Not one little bit, Wat," said Theo. He flicked through the aluminium book, pretending to study.

Wat stayed looking at him for a moment, then started to walk away. He stopped after a few paces and looked back.

"I'll say you'll *think* about it?" he asked.

Theo tried to ignore him.

When Wat had gone, Theo couldn't concentrate. Bauxite could come from the moon for all he cared. He couldn't stop thinking about Captain Cringle's Tower. What had his grandfather meant, "it was for everybody"?

Wat's bit of paper was still lying on the desk. Theo

looked at it, then stood up and walked over to the librarian.

"Excuse me, I'm looking for a book," began Theo.

"Yes?" said the librarian, looking up from her computer screen. "What's the author's name?"

"Brusset," said Theo.

The librarian typed in the name and watched the screen.

"Ah, here we are," she said, brightly. "*The Cringle Bequest*, by the Reverend Algernon Brusset, vicar of St Stephen's, Bunting, 1873." The librarian's face fell. "Oh, I'm sorry. I'm afraid it's not available. It's got 'GM' next to it – that means 'Gone Missing'."

So that's that, thought Theo.

"Why are you interested?" asked the librarian.

"To do with the tower," said Theo.

"Oh, the one they're going to demolish?"

"That's it. There's something on it in that book."

"There are some books on Bunting in the Local History section."

"Thanks, but that was the one that really interested me."

"Perhaps it will turn up," said the librarian.

"Yes, perhaps," said Theo. "Thanks."

Theo went back to his project but he couldn't

concentrate. He'd still only written four words. He decided there was no point in staying any longer and that he'd go home. He put the aluminium book back on the shelf and picked up his bag.

As he was walking out past the library desks the alarm went off.

That'll be Wat, thought Theo crossly. Wat was always setting off alarms. Theo wondered if he'd done it on purpose this time.

"I've not got any books," he said, showing the librarian his things.

"That's all right," said the librarian. "There's something wrong with the alarm. It's always going off like that."

When Theo came out of the library it was still raining. The water swirled across the pavement and large puddles had formed at the sides of the road. Not in the mood for waiting, he put up his hood and strode out into the wet.

As he was walking up the hill away from the library, he passed a paper shop. A board outside caught his eye. In bold black letters it said "TOWER PLANS ENRAGE LOCALS". Theo went into the shop to take a quick look at the newspaper.

There was a report on the front page. But it wasn't quite the public outcry that the headline suggested. A woman who walked her dog along the cliff path said that it was "a bit of a shame". And another person said demolishing the tower would "spoil the view".

And that was it. The article finished by saying that the plans could be inspected at the council offices and the planning committee would meet at the town hall to discuss the project at three p.m. on Wednesday. Members of the public were welcome.

Theo left the shop and continued walking. The rain had eased and soon stopped altogether. The storm clouds began to break up and there was even a bit of blue sky showing.

He started thinking about the planning meeting. Perhaps it would be interesting to go along. He felt sure that the muted response from people was partly because they were afraid to criticize Josiah Jellicon. As the biggest employer in the neighbourhood he was a powerful and important man. It was understandable that people were reluctant to speak out. Theo's own father worked at the Jellicon Comestibles factory and he wouldn't hear a bad word said about his employer.

However, Theo felt a bit differently. He thought that Jellicon took advantage of his position and did things that perhaps he shouldn't. He was sure Jellicon wasn't quite the generous man and kind employer that he liked people to think he was.

And what about what his grandfather had told Wat? That the tower had been "for everyone"? If it was true, and Captain Cringle had left the tower to the whole town, then Jellicon was wrong to knock it down.

The more Theo thought about it, the more he thought that perhaps he would see what he could do to save the tower. He could go along to the planning meeting. It was a public meeting after all. He could just see what was happening. Perhaps he would ask a question about the Captain Cringle story. He didn't have to do any more than that. He didn't have to get involved in anything else. There'd be no harm in going. He'd have every right to be there.

At least that way he wouldn't be confronting Jellicon directly. That was the thing he most wanted to avoid.

As Theo walked along, a large metallic-red car sped towards him. It was a brand new Bentley Continental GT. As Theo stood admiring it, he glimpsed the man at the wheel. It was Josiah Jellicon.

As the car sped past, its wheels went through a large puddle at the side of the road. An enormous jet of water sprayed up and across the pavement and drenched Theo with muddy water.

Theo thought he saw the hint of a smile on Jellicon's face. Had Jellicon recognized him? He wasn't sure. If he had, then perhaps he'd soaked Theo deliberately. Theo wouldn't put it past a man like Jellicon. That made him angry. Jellicon just did what he wanted, without caring about anybody else. Why should he get away with it? Theo determined to speak out at the planning meeting.

"Hey, you look cross!"

Theo looked round, wondering where the voice had come from. There didn't seem to be anyone about. Then he spotted a black-clothed figure with pink hair, sitting on the branch of a tree. It was the not-really-dead girl, Alix.

"Oh, no! Not you!" groaned Theo.

"Charming toad," said Alix, sticking out her tongue. "Here, *and* you're wet! What happened?"

"Jellicon, that's what," said Theo. "Just ran through a puddle in his new car and soaked me."

"He he! Nice one!" laughed Alix, nearly falling off her branch.

"So how come they let you out?" said Theo, crossly. Alix, who had got to Deadland by mistake, was looked after by LIMBO, the Lost Infants and Motherless Babies Organization. Theo's grandma had something to do with it but Theo didn't know quite what.

**45**

"I was *told* to come," said Alix, jumping off the branch. "'Cause I'm *special*!"

"Like bananas, you are!" said Theo.

"I am. I can do what I want." Alix flounced about on the bit of grass under the tree. "And guess what?"

"Grandma sent you," said Theo, flatly.

Alix stopped prancing about. "How d'you know that?"

"I'm not stupid," said Theo. "Unlike some—"

"All right, all right," cried Alix, looking fierce. "So *are* you going to do anything about it?"

"What, the tower?"

"Of course the tower, you haddock."

"Not much," said Theo. "But I'll go to the planning meeting."

"That'll please your grandma."

"It had better," said Theo, "because I'm not doing anything else."

"I'll tell her," said Alix.

The town hall clock struck three.

"Yikes, is that the time?" cried Alix. "I'm late! She'll murder me!" And setting off at a run, she disappeared down the road.

If you are going to do some public speaking, it is a good idea to be prepared. It's no good standing up and saying the first thing that comes into your head. You need to decide beforehand what you're going to say. If you don't, you might talk gibberish. That would be bad enough. Much worse, you might say nothing at all.

Theo had never done any public speaking. He'd decided that he was going to speak at the planning meeting so he thought that he had better do some preparation. He was only going to ask a question but he still wanted to get it right. It would be no good standing up only to make a fool of himself.

Theo wrote out his question on a bit of paper. He then wrote it out a second time on another bit of paper in case the first piece got lost. And then, to make extra sure, he wrote the question out again on his left hand. That way he thought he'd be safe.

After lunch on Wednesday, Theo got ready to go out. He put on his best trousers. He thought it would be a good idea to create the right impression.

"Why Theo, you're looking smart!" said Mrs Slugg.

"I expect he's going to meet someone," said Louise.

"A girl!" shrieked Clare. "Theo's going to meet a girl."

"I'm not!" said Theo, going pink.

"It's all right, Theo, you don't have to tell us where you're off to," said Mrs Slugg.

"If you must know, I'm going to the town hall," said Theo.

"Why are you going there?"

"To the planning meeting. They're going to discuss Cringle's Tower."

"But I thought you didn't care about it being knocked down?" said Louise.

"I don't," said Theo. "I'm just interested."

When Theo arrived at the town hall, he was shown to the meeting room. He sat with a few other people, none of whom he recognized. There didn't seem to be much interest in the proceedings. Opposite, there was a row of desks behind which the committee members sat. To one side a man was sorting through a large stack of papers. A label on his desk said that he was the planning officer. And on the other side there were two empty chairs. Theo wondered when the meeting was going to start.

The committee members kept muttering to each other and looking at their watches. It was obvious that they wanted to get going but that they were waiting for somebody. At last the door opened and in walked Mr and Mrs Jellicon. Everybody stood up. Even Theo couldn't help it.

Mr Jellicon beamed at the room in general and shook hands vigorously with the planning officer and various members of the committee. Mrs Jellicon smiled and held out her hand to one or two special people. It was the first time Theo had seen her close to. She was a tall woman with blonde hair and she smiled a lot. When she'd finished shaking hands everybody sat down and the meeting began.

The planning officer stopped sorting his papers and stood up.

"Could we have the blinds down on the windows, please?" he said. "And then the first slide? Thank you."

Somebody pulled down the window blinds, the room became dark and then the slide show began. The first picture was of Cringle's Tower. It was upside down.

"Sorry!" said the man operating the projector. He hurriedly put the slide up the right way.

The planning officer cleared his throat and then started talking. "This is Cringle's Tower," he began.

"Woe! Woe!" came a wailing that Theo knew only too well. Mrs Cringle entered the room through the wall behind the slide screen. Theo wondered how on earth he was going to concentrate with her wailing and waving. She walked backwards into the middle of the room, her one eye gazing at the picture on the screen.

Then a movement caught Theo's eye. It was Mrs Jellicon's handkerchief, which she held in her right hand, and it stood out clearly in the darkness. She shook it casually but Theo could see that actually she was signalling to a man standing behind her.

Theo stared. The man was a ghost. There was no doubt about it; the same bluish glow that Grandma and the other ghosts all had was clearly visible in the darkness. He was smartly dressed in a long tailcoat but he looked like a thug. Theo shivered. He didn't like the look of this.

The man nodded slightly at Mrs Jellicon as if he understood what she wanted and stepped forward. The moment Mrs Cringle saw him, she stopped wailing and her mouth dropped open. She started backing away but the man grabbed her and dragged her out of the room straight through the slide screen.

Theo was shocked. He didn't know what to make of it. He looked at Mrs Jellicon and glimpsed her half smile in the darkness. What was going on? Mrs Jellicon could see ghosts – and they did things for her! The thought so alarmed Theo that for a few minutes he couldn't concentrate on the proceedings.

Theo managed to pull himself together. The planning officer had continued talking, oblivious to what had been going on. He was describing how the crumbling tower was a danger to the public and how Mr Jellicon's new scheme would greatly enhance the area and provide a much needed boost to the community. There followed lots of slides of what the new golf clubhouse and restaurant would look like and the planning officer used phrases such as "sympathetic to the environment" and "sensitive landscaping".

Theo started to get bored. It all seemed to be taking a very long time. Then suddenly the blinds were up, the room was full of light and he heard the planning officer say, "And now members of the public can speak if they wish to. Please limit your comments to three minutes."

Theo sat up and looked about, hoping that somebody else would be the first to speak. He recognized the librarian, Miss Sheldon, sitting at the back of the room. He hadn't noticed her before and thought she must have come in late. She didn't seem to want to say anything. Nobody did. Everyone sat looking sullen. They didn't budge.

Theo took a deep breath. He stuck up his hand. The planning officer nodded at him encouragingly. Theo stood up, shakily.

Then he remembered that he needed his bits of paper. He stuck his hands in his pockets, searching for them. He couldn't find them. He searched all his pockets. It was no good, somehow they had got lost. Perhaps he'd left them in his other trousers. Trying not to panic, Theo looked at his left hand. The writing had got a bit smudged but he could just make it out. He took another deep breath. Then he caught sight of Mr Jellicon looking at him.

He looked furious. He'd obviously recognized Theo.

"Surely you're not going to allow questions from a . . . a . . . mere schoolboy?" barked Jellicon.

Theo was shaking like a leaf. He nearly sat down there and then.

Mrs Jellicon smiled serenely and took her husband's hand.

"I don't see why not," said the planning officer, boldly. "This is a public meeting." He turned back to Theo. "Did you want to say something?" He gave Theo another nod.

Josiah Jellicon had gone purple. The man looked about to explode. His wife patted him on the arm.

Theo tried to speak. For a moment no sound came out. When it finally did, his voice was high-pitched and squeaky. "Er . . . there's a story that Captain Cringle gave the tower to everybody who lives in Bunting. If this is true, shouldn't it be saved and not knocked down?"

"I've not heard that story," said the planning officer. "Have you ever heard of such a thing, Mr Jellicon?"

Josiah Jellicon shook his head. "No, no, never. I've never heard of anything like that." He still looked fierce and Theo could tell he was straining to keep his voice even. Was he telling the truth?

**53**

"But if there was, there'd be no question of knocking the tower down?" said Theo. He spoke without thinking. He hadn't written the words down and wondered later where they had come from, and his courage to say them.

"Certainly not," said Mr Jellicon, still struggling to keep his temper. "If there had been such a stipulation, then of course the tower would remain. Indeed, I would restore it for the benefit of the local inhabitants."

Everybody on the committee smiled at Mr Jellicon's generosity. They also looked rather relieved.

Theo sat down.

"Thank you," said the planning officer. "Then, if there are no more questions, we'll put it to the vote."

All the committee put up their hands.

The application was passed. The tower would be knocked down.

The meeting over, everybody got up to leave. Theo made for the door. He didn't want to hang around with the Jellicons in the room, especially after what had happened. But as he waited for an elderly man who was in front of him, someone gripped his arm tightly. Theo swung round and met Mrs Jellicon's gaze.

"What an interesting question you asked," she said, slowly releasing her grip. "I'm *so* glad you came to the meeting." She smiled but her smile had no warmth to it. It seemed venomous, like a snake's, thought Theo.

He smiled politely but didn't say anything.

"You're a bold boy, and could go far," said Mrs Jellicon, regarding him with her cold blue eyes. "It will be fascinating to watch your progress."

Theo had·an uncomfortable feeling that Mrs Jellicon really meant something else. As if she was telling him to beware.

"Lola? Lola, darling?" Josiah Jellicon called. He was busy talking to some of the committee members and hadn't seen Theo. Mrs Jellicon gave Theo a sharp glance and turned back to her husband. "Ah, there you are, Lola. I'd like you to meet Adam Richards, the new mayor. He's invited us to a soirée tomorrow."

"Mr Richards, how lovely," purred Mrs Jellicon.

Theo hurried through the door.

"Hey, excuse me. Wait a moment!" called a voice as Theo was going down the town hall steps. He turned and saw the librarian, Miss Sheldon, coming after him. He waited for her to catch up.

"Hello," said Theo. "I saw you at the meeting."

"Yes, I came in late after the slides had started. I just wanted to say I was interested in what you said," said the librarian. "Is that why you wanted the Brusset book? Did you think it might have something on the story of the tower?"

"Er . . . yes, I was told it might have," answered Theo.

"I was thinking . . . I could search for it, if you like.

Books do get misplaced and quite a few entries are wrong in the catalogue. The new computer system took some doing and mistakes were made, I'm afraid."

"Thanks," said Theo. "That's really kind. But isn't it too late, now the plans have been passed?"

"Hmm, I take your point," said the librarian. "But the tower's still standing. I heard Mr Jellicon say to the planning officer that the demolition would be arranged for Monday. That gives us a little time."

"All right," said Theo. "If it's not too much trouble."

As Theo walked home he wondered about what had happened at the meeting. He didn't know what to make of Mrs Jellicon and the ghost. It had never occurred to him that someone else might be able to see ghosts, let alone actually control them as Mrs Jellicon had done. What had become of Mrs Cringle?

And what about Mr Jellicon's behaviour? He had certainly been furious that Theo had dared to speak. But was that all? Was it simply that he was so determined to get his own way that anybody who stood up to him or looked like upsetting his plans made him cross? Theo wasn't sure. He wondered if perhaps Jellicon was hiding something. He certainly seemed anxious to do everything properly. Was he *too* anxious? Was he worried that people might start asking awkward questions? Perhaps there was something about Captain Cringle's tower that the Jellicons were keeping secret. Theo wished he could have seen a copy of the book his grandfather had mentioned. Perhaps the librarian would find it. Perhaps. . .

But eventually Theo decided there was no point in thinking any more about it. He couldn't see that it would make any difference; Jellicon was sure to have an explanation for everything. Theo had done what he could. Surely his grandma would see that?

When Theo got home he was disgusted to find that the little black birds were still dancing about on his television screen. But as he watched, they all danced gradually off to the sides and a message appeared:

> *Dear Theo,*
> *Come to Deadland tonight at 10 p.m.*
> *love Grandma*

*Love* Grandma? Was this a joke? Theo was suspicious. What was she up to now?

The words stayed on the screen for two minutes

and then disappeared. To Theo's delight they were replaced by the control room of the Starship *Explorer*. His television and video games were all working again.

Theo wasn't at all keen about going to Deadland. As ten o'clock approached, he began to seriously think that he wouldn't go. Who'd choose to visit a lot of dead people? The place really gave him the creeps. But he knew that if he didn't go then Grandma would come to him. There'd be no avoiding her. On this occasion it seemed simpler to do as she asked.

At five to ten Theo switched off his television. He went over to the lift buttons and after a moment's hesitation pressed the button for the basement. The lift started travelling downwards.

There was a "ping" as the lift stopped at the first floor. The doors opened and there were Mrs Trillaby and her dog.

"Hello, Mrs Trillaby. How are you?" said Theo.

"Oh, there's no end to it," said Mrs Trillaby. "Look at my hair! Is that what you'd call stylish?"

Theo thought Mrs Trillaby's hair made it look as though her head was covered in bubbles. Mrs Trillaby was always having trouble with her hair. She changed hairdressers like other people changed underwear.

"Oh dear!" said Theo, trying to sound concerned.

Mrs Trillaby nodded agreement. "Exactly. I'm not going to stand for it. I've a good mind to go to another salon straight away. And I thought Ronnie was such a nice boy."

The dog, which was small and looked like a mop, was sniffing around Theo's feet. He seemed to be looking for something. Theo shifted uncomfortably. He wished the lift would hurry up and reach the ground floor. He wasn't in the mood for Mrs Trillaby's hair or her dog.

At last the lift stopped and the doors opened. Mrs Trillaby and her dog hurried straight out.

"Oh dear," said Mrs Trillaby, looking round. "This isn't right. Where are we? Oh, not there, Pixie! Naughty boy!" She hurried back into the lift, dragging the dog by his lead. Pixie slid across the floor, leaving a suspiciously damp trail.

With a shock Theo saw that outside all was darkness. They must have gone past the ground floor without stopping. They'd arrived in Deadland.

"This lift isn't serviced often enough," said Mrs Trillaby, apparently none the worse for her visit to the Land of the Dead. She gave the button for the ground floor a firm push. "I shall have a word with Mr Windrush about it."

When they reached the ground floor, Theo watched as Mrs Trillaby and Pixie set off for their evening walk. Stepping carefully to avoid the wet patch on the floor, he again pressed the button for the basement.

The lift travelled downwards.

"Late as usual," said Grandma when she met Theo in the darkness.

"It was Mrs Trillaby, she got into the –" began Theo but his grandma wasn't listening. She had turned and was hobbling away.

"I want you to see something," she said.

They walked for a minute or two and then Theo saw what looked like a huddle of clothes on the ground. As he got closer he realized it was Mrs Cringle, sitting hunched up. She looked in a bad way, as if she'd had a big shock. She shrunk back as they approached.

"Wat Kemp found her," said Grandma. "She'd been dumped back here in this state. I can't get any sense from her. She's a complete wreck."

"What happened?" asked Theo, wondering if it

was *ever* possible to get sense from Mrs Cringle.

"I was hoping you'd tell me that," said Grandma. "You *were* at the meeting, weren't you?"

"Yes, of course!" said Theo, suddenly putting the facts together. He stared at Mrs Cringle. Had that other ghost done this? "There was a man – a ghost – there. He stopped Mrs Cringle wailing and carried her away."

"What was he like?"

"A big man, dressed in a long tailcoat. He was with the Jellicons. Mrs Jellicon – she could see him!"

"Hmm," said Grandma grimly. "Then it's worse than I thought."

"The man, do you know him?"

"If it's who I think it is, his name's Drake. He used to be butler to Mr Jellicon's grandfather. An ugly brute."

"That sounds like him," said Theo. "I think –"

"You think what?"

"I think Jellicon might be hiding something. The committee passed the plans but I'm sure that Jellicon knew about the story and was pretending he didn't. Perhaps if—"

"No," broke in Grandma. "Leave it now. You can't do any more. The tower will be demolished."

"But Grandma," persisted Theo, "Jellicon shouldn't get away with it!"

"Leave it! You little idiot. The man's dangerous!" said Grandma.

"Jellicon?"

"No, Drake," sighed Grandma.

"Why?" asked Theo. "He's just a ghost."

"Yes, he's just a ghost but he's on *their* side, isn't he? That makes a difference." She helped Mrs Cringle to her feet. The two of them started hobbling away. "Leave it alone, Theo. Go home."

Theo turned and made his way back to the lift.

He couldn't make it out. What was she on about? So what if the ghost was on their side, why should that matter to him? His grandma had wanted his help and now, when he was actually quite keen to do something, she wasn't interested. Was there no pleasing her?

Back in the lift, he sat down on his bed. He pulled off his shoes and stood up to take off his clothes. He was tired and ready for sleep. He took a deep breath and sighed.

He sniffed.

"What the –?" muttered Theo.

He was standing in a puddle of something smelly.

And then he remembered Mrs Trillaby's dog.

Next morning, Theo rose early to get into the bath-room before his sisters. Despite washing his feet the previous night, the smell of Mrs Trillaby's dog seemed to linger. He washed thoroughly, brushed his teeth, and then stood studying his face in the mirror.

He started thinking again about his grandma and the fact that she didn't want him to do any more about the tower. He couldn't understand why she wanted him to leave off now, just when he thought Jellicon was hiding something and he was prepared to do some investigating. The demolition wasn't until Monday. There was still time to stop it.

But then Theo came to his senses. Jellicon wasn't a man you'd choose to argue with if you didn't have to. He expected to get his own way, Theo could see that.

And Theo didn't really care about the tower. What difference would it make, knocking it down? Not much. His grandma wanted him to stay out of it. So this time, he'd do as she said. Then perhaps – although it seemed unlikely – she'd leave him alone for good. That was what Theo wanted most of all.

Theo noticed that he had a small pimple on the end of his nose. He bent towards the mirror to look at it more closely. To his surprise and alarm the pimple started to grow before his eyes. It became bigger and bigger, a sharp black point like a bird's beak. Then suddenly Theo realized that it *was* a bird's beak, pushing through the mirror in front of him. Theo stumbled backwards as a large black crow flew into the room.

The crow flew about the tiny bathroom squawking madly. It settled on top of a cupboard and started knocking down his mother's little bottles of cosmetics. One rolled off the shelf and Theo only just managed to catch it before it hit the floor.

"Stop!" cried Theo, waving his hands. He jumped up and tried to grab the bird but it dodged him, flying off around the room.

"Krark!" squawked the crow.

"Krark, krark" came more squawks from the

basin as another crow pushed into the room. It flew over to the toilet roll and began pecking at the paper.

"Oh no!" groaned Theo. "Get out! Get out!"

Theo waved his arms about, trying to catch the crows but they spun around him in a whirling mass of feathers. The crows then started to have an argument with the toilet paper, pulling the roll, until the whole thing had unravelled all around the room.

"Stop!" shouted Theo. "Stop!" He tried to catch the birds but somehow they just managed to avoid his fingers.

Theo saw a smudge of bright pink in the mirror. It resolved into the spiky hair of Alix, the not-really-dead girl.

"Oh, no, not *you* again!" moaned Theo. "I might have guessed!"

Alix climbed through the mirror into the bathroom, her black boots treading in the basin.

"Pleased to see me?" she grinned, sticking out her tongue.

"Like I'm pleased to see a rotten egg," said Theo. "I suppose Grandma sent you."

"No, I came on my own," said Alix.

"Do you think I'm stupid?" said Theo. "I don't believe you."

"Believe what you like. It's true."

The crows, who had draped the whole roll of toilet paper about the room, went back to knocking things off the shelves.

"Arghh!" cried Theo, rushing forwards. "Are these birds yours? Can't you stop them?"

"They're not doing any harm," said Alix. "They're excited, it's their first visit."

Theo did his best to catch falling bottles and jars.

"*Pleeease* stop them!" he shouted.

Alix put two fingers into her mouth and let out a piercing whistle. The two crows instantly flew to her and settled on her shoulders.

Theo stood looking at the mess.

Someone rapped on the bathroom door. "How long are you going to be in there?" called Kate, the eldest of Theo's sisters.

"Sorry, I won't be long," replied Theo.

"Well hurry up, I'm late already!" cried Kate.

Theo started gathering up the toilet paper. He tried rolling it back on the roll but that took ages so he decided to shove it down the toilet instead. "You choose your moments," he hissed at Alix.

Alix grinned. The two crows stared at Theo with their black beady eyes.

"What are you here for, anyway?" asked Theo. "The tower's going to be knocked down. Jellicon had it all sewn up beforehand."

"But Jellicon's up to something. You know that."

"Maybe he is but I can't see what we can do about it."

"We could look for evidence," said Alix.

"What do you expect to find? Jellicon is hardly likely to leave anything lying about."

"We could still look. He shouldn't get away with it."

"You can if you want but I'm not," said Theo. He was determined to stay out of it. "I did what I could. Now go away."

"You're chicken!" said Alix.

"No I'm not!" said Theo. "Grandma said not to."

"Oh, so we're a good little boy now, are we?"

"She said not to because of the ghost, Drake," said Theo. "She said he's dangerous."

"A ghost?" sneered Alix. "Peew! Who cares about a ghost!"

"And Mrs Jellicon can see ghosts," said Theo. "She'll see you."

"Not if she's not there she won't," replied Alix. "I expect they're always going out. I'll just wait until they do."

"Go on, then. Now, please go away!" cried Theo. "And take your blinking birds with you!" The crows had started to fly about the bathroom again.

"Theo!" came Kate's voice from outside the bathroom. "Why are you talking to yourself? Stop it and hurry up!"

Alix climbed back through the mirror. Halfway through, she turned round.

"Well I'm going to go to Jellicon's house to investigate. If you had any guts you'd come too."

"Go away," hissed Theo. "And don't come back!"

"Chicken!" said Alix.

"Krark, krark!" squawked the crows.

"THEO!" shouted Kate, hammering her fists on the bathroom door.

"All right, all right!" Theo shouted back.

He shoved the last bit of toilet paper into the toilet and pressed the flush.

"Oh, no!" he groaned as the water filled to the brim and then began to overflow on to the floor.

"Theo, what a mess!" cried Mrs Slugg, when she saw the bathroom. "What on earth's been happening? It looks like a hurricane's been in here."

"Sorry, Mum," said Theo. "A . . . a bird got in through the skylight and I couldn't catch it."

"A bird? How did it do that?" said Mrs Slugg, looking doubtfully at the ceiling. "And the floor's all wet."

"Don't worry, Mum. I'll clean up," said Theo and, sighing, he went to get the cleaning things.

Theo decided to spend the rest of the day in the lift. It seemed the best place to keep out of trouble. He thought he'd play a video game for an hour or so and then do some more work on his school project. By the end of the day, he'd written almost half a page.

Shortly after nine o'clock, Theo's dad got into the lift. He was carrying a large black bag full of rubbish. He peeped around Theo's curtain.

"Working hard as usual?" said Mr Slugg, with a grin.

"Hello, Dad," said Theo, who had just reached level 49 in Starship *Explorer*. "Aluminium's so *boring*."

"Maybe, but it's good for recycling," said Mr Slugg, putting down the rubbish bag in front of Theo.

"All right, Dad, I'll take it down," he said.

As Theo came back from dumping the rubbish in the bins at the back of Vanilla Villas, he heard a strange noise. It was a sort of drumming, a bit like thunder, and was getting louder and louder.

It was almost dark and Theo peered down the road in front of him wondering what it could be. Then around the corner at the far end of the road he saw four black horses come galloping at a terrific speed. Behind them they pulled a large black coach.

As they approached, Theo saw two of the horses brush through some bushes at the edge of the road. Next they seemed to charge straight through a lamp-post. And then, as they got closer and closer, Theo could see the faintest hint of a blue glow about them.

Theo stared, open-mouthed, as the truth dawned on him. They were ghost horses and the coach they were pulling was a phantom coach. On top of the coach, bouncing precariously on the coachman's box and looking as though she might fall off at any moment, was a small figure with bright pink hair. . .

"Oh, blimey!" muttered Theo as he realized that they were heading straight towards him. Would the phantom horses and coach pass straight through him? He wasn't going to stay around to find out. He started to run for the entrance to Vanilla Villas but it was no good, he knew he wasn't going to make it. In desperation he threw himself flat on the ground. He was only just in time as the horses and the coach thundered over his head. There was a cloud of dust and a chilling rush of wind, then the horses pulled up and the coach squealed to a stop.

"Wow!" shouted Alix, jumping down from her perch on the coach. "That was fun!"

Theo struggled to his feet, shaking.

"It might have been fun for you!" he gasped, trying to get his breath back. "But I was very nearly run over by a phantom coach-and-four. Where did you get this thing? What are you doing?"

"I borrowed it. I'm going to Jellicon's house, of

course!" said Alix, grinning. Then she gave Theo a sly look and said, "Come too!"

"What, with those things?" said Theo, looking at the horses. He'd always been a bit afraid of horses and, as you might expect, these were no exceptions. He didn't like the wild look in their eyes. "No way!"

"Oh, go on," said Alix. "You could. . . You could tell me the way while I drive the horses. . ."

"Oh, I get it!" cried Theo. "You don't know the way."

"Yes I do!" protested Alix.

"No, you don't," said Theo. "That's why you've come here, isn't it?"

Alix looked awkward and said nothing.

"Well, I'm not coming," said Theo. "But I'll get you a map. You can find your way with that. The house is called The Magnolias."

"Go on," pleaded Alix. "See if you can get into the coach. It'll be fun."

"That thing? You've got to be joking!"

"Why not?" said Alix.

"No," said Theo, stubbornly.

"Just try," said Alix.

"Ummm," pondered Theo.

"You don't have to come. Just see if you can get in."

"Oh, all right," said Theo, at last. "But I bet it doesn't work. . ."

He went to the side of the coach and tried putting a foot on the step. He could just feel it, as if he were touching the surface of the water in a swimming pool, but then his foot sunk through.

"There," he said, "I knew it wouldn't work. I'll go and get a map."

"Couldn't you come another way?" said Alix. "Walk or something?"

"Walk? What, behind this thing? At the speed you go? Don't make me laugh!"

"I'll go slowly."

Theo looked dubious.

"Really, really slowly," said Alix. "And we'll only go near the house if they're out."

Theo thought about it. It might be worth a try. He realized that he was still keen to see if Jellicon was up to something. The Jellicons lived on the outskirts of a small village about five miles from Bunting. Theo wasn't exactly sure where the house was but he reckoned he could find it. It wasn't far. If he cycled they could get there quite quickly.

"You're sure you can make those things go slowly?" asked Theo, looking anxiously at the horses.

"Yes," nodded Alix, looking miserable at the thought of it.

"OK, I'll ride my bicycle. You'll have to follow along behind." Theo wasn't sure it would work but supposed it was worth trying. He fetched his bicycle from the garage at the back of Vanilla Villas and they set off.

Theo felt rather strange as they made their way through the gathering dusk into the countryside. He could hear the horses close behind him and could feel their chilly breath on his neck. But now and then, when a car came up behind and its headlights cast a shadow of only him on his bicycle, he'd wonder if the coach was still there, and the moment the car had passed he'd turn round to check. To his relief, it always was, with Alix perched on top and holding tightly to the reins.

They reached the village. As they passed the pub, a group of people came out of the door. They were chatting loudly but fell silent as Theo cycled past. He kept his head down, wondering if they could see the phantom coach.

"Are we nearly there?" yelled Alix, when they had left the village behind.

"Just about," shouted Theo over his shoulder. He

pulled up at a road junction. The road divided in two, one road went downhill, the other went uphill. Theo hadn't the faintest idea which to take.

"I thought you knew the way!" cried Alix.

"I do!" shouted Theo. "It's this way." He pointed uphill.

"All right then," said Alix and she waved the whip at the horses. They started immediately uphill.

Theo struggled after them. When he eventually reached the top, Alix was looking about. The road had become a farm track, ending in a farmyard. The horses were quite excited and started neighing. Thank goodness they're ghosts, thought Theo, at least the farm animals won't hear them.

But Theo had hardly had the thought before some horses in the stables started neighing and kicking their stalls. Then the whole farmyard joined in – a cockerel started crowing, a donkey braying and some pigs oinking. Finally a large dog awoke and dashed from its kennel on the end of a chain, barking furiously.

"So is this where Jellicon lives?" bellowed Alix above the racket.

"Of course it's not!" cried Theo. "Let's get out of here before someone comes."

But at that moment the farmhouse door opened

and light flooded into the yard. The whole farmyard of animals instantly fell silent, except for the vile dog, who stopped barking and emitted low and menacing growls.

"Oi, you!" bawled a voice that grated like a tractor's gearbox. "Stop!"

A short, brawny man stood in the doorway. He stood with his feet apart, like a wrestler about to spring, and in his hands he held a colossal pitchfork, at least two and a half metres long. Theo had never seen anything like it; feeling a chill in the pit of his stomach, he realized that it was pointing straight at him.

"Move an inch and you'll be stuck full of holes like a sausage!" growled the farmer. "Hmm, might fry you as well." The dog, straining at the end of its chain a few metres from Theo, continued to snarl.

Theo, who suddenly felt very much on his own despite the fact that he was surrounded by phantoms, stood as still as a statue. He stared into the light, hoping that the farmer would not jab him with the pitchfork.

"Anyway, what are you doing, prowling around here?"

"I'm lost," whimpered Theo. "I'm just trying to get home." He hoped that he didn't look like a burglar.

"A likely story! I know your sort, up to no good, skulking around people's houses in the dead of night."

"I . . . I'm not. . ." mumbled Theo.

"What is it, Cecil? What's going on?" a woman's voice called from inside the house. The voice seemed vaguely familiar but Theo couldn't think why. A plumpish woman appeared behind the farmer.

"Caught this ruffian about to steal my prize turkeys," said the farmer gruffly.

"Really?" said the woman, peering at Theo over the farmer's shoulder. "He doesn't look like a turkey rustler. . ."

The farmer dropped the pitchfork a little. The dog stopped growling.

Theo tried to think good thoughts in an effort to look as innocent as possible.

"No," said the farmer's wife, stepping in front of her husband. "I'm sure I've seen him. . ."

"You think so?" said the farmer, sounding disappointed.

"Oh, of course I know him!" cried his wife. "You chump, Cecil Plimpton! That's no ruffian. That's the Slugg sisters' elder brother what used to be at Tolley's School. Given him his dinner many a time."

Then Theo remembered. It was Mrs Plimpton, the dinner lady from his old school.

"Hello Mrs Plimpton!" he cried, almost sinking to

**79**

his knees in relief as the farmer put down the pitch-fork. "I got lost on a cycle ride – I'm only trying to get home. But it's all right. I know the way now."

"Wait a moment," said Mrs Plimpton. She disappeared into the house and a moment later reappeared with something wrapped up in foil.

"A little piece of fruitcake to help you on your journey home," she said with a broad smile. "Poor dear, you getting a fright like that."

"Thank you, Mrs Plimpton," said Theo.

"Take care on your way back down the track," said the farmer, looking miserable.

Theo waved goodbye and started off towards the farm gate. It was only when he was cycling down the track that he noticed that there was no sign of Alix, the phantom horses or the coach. They had all disappeared.

# 13

Now that Alix had taken off on her own, Theo was tempted to cycle straight home. His experience with the farmer had shaken him and he was again having doubts about breaking into the Jellicons' house. Jellicon was far too smart to leave any incriminating evidence just lying around. And what if someone was to catch them at the house? The whole plan looked decidedly risky.

Theo even got so far as to start off back along the road to Bunting. But after a few metres he slammed on the brakes and skidded to a stop. What if there *was* some evidence? What if Jellicon had deliberately deceived the Planning Committee? Having come all this way, was he really going to run straight home leaving Alix to take all the credit for thwarting Jellicon?

Theo turned around and cycled back to the road junction. There he took the other turning and within five minutes reached the gateway of a large house. There was a carved stone plaque beside the gates which said it was The Magnolias. It was the house where Mr and Mrs Jellicon lived.

Although The Magnolias looked old, it had only been built a few years before. Josiah Jellicon had knocked down a perfectly good house and then built what he thought would be a more suitable residence for a man as rich and successful as he was. It had everything, including gates which remained firmly shut unless you were an expected visitor.

Having hidden his bicycle in some bushes, Theo kept close to the wall in case there were security cameras around. But the Jellicons didn't seem especially worried about intruders. The wall was not a very high one and Theo had no difficulty in climbing over. He dropped down into the bushes on the other side and crept into the garden.

The house was surrounded by lawns with clumps of trees and shrubs. To one side was a small lake. Theo kept his eyes open for Alix but there was no sign of her or the phantom coach. Theo wondered where they'd got to. Surely they hadn't got lost? Or perhaps

Alix had lost her nerve and gone back to Deadland.

Theo saw that the Jellicons' red Bentley was parked in front of the house. So they hadn't gone out yet. Theo wondered whether they would.

Keeping to the shadows, he skirted the house looking up at the windows. There were lots of lights on. He caught sight of the Jellicons in an upstairs room. Mrs Jellicon appeared to be adjusting her make-up and Mr Jellicon was walking back and forth, talking on the telephone. Theo could just hear the murmur of his voice.

He moved behind a patch of bushes and felt something cold brush against his ankle.

"Hey, look where you're walking!" hissed Alix.

"Oh, you're here!" said Theo, crouching down.

"Course I'm here," whispered Alix. "And keep your voice down."

"You might have warned me!" said Theo.

"I was watching the house, you pollack. Waiting for them to go out. What took you so long?"

Theo could see that Alix was grinning in the darkness. He couldn't think how he hadn't seen her. Her pink hair seemed to be positively glowing with excitement.

"You know what took me so long!" he muttered. He didn't tell her that he'd nearly gone straight home.

He was almost beginning to wish he had. He'd hoped the house would be empty. The sight of the Jellicons made him uncomfortable. That and the fact that Alix was obviously enjoying herself.

At the house, the lights were switched off one by one, then the front door opened and out came Josiah Jellicon.

"Come on, Lola darling," he called. "We should get there before the dessert, you know." He sauntered over to the Bentley. There was a high-pitched "peep" as the doors unlocked.

Mrs Jellicon appeared, closed the door, walked down the front steps and got into the car. Josiah Jellicon started the engine and the Bentley purred down the drive. As it reached the gates they opened automatically and closed again after the car had passed through. Theo watched the car's headlights until they disappeared down the lane.

"Good. Now then, let's see if we can get into the house," said Alix.

"Wait, aren't you forgetting something?" said Theo.

"What?"

"There's a ghost, isn't there? Drake. Grandma said—"

"Yes, I know," said Alix. "I'll be careful."

They walked cautiously towards the darkened house. Theo was suspicious. It seemed odd that there was no security lighting. Surely there was at least a burglar alarm? He was thankful that Wat wasn't with them. If he had been then the bells would surely have been ringing by now. But perhaps there weren't any bells, just an alarm connected directly to the police station and the police would turn up at any moment and arrest them. He remembered that it would only be him that would have to spend the night in a police cell.

"I'll go in and see if I can unlock the door from the other side," whispered Alix.

"OK," said Theo.

Theo watched while Alix walked through the door. He saw her put up her hand and push through, just as if the door had been a curtain. There was a strange swishing noise as she went through. She disappeared into the house.

Theo waited. The minutes ticked by but Alix didn't reappear. Where had she got to? Couldn't she manage the lock? She didn't have the strength of a live person.

He walked around to the side of the house where

there were some French doors. He was about to peer in when he heard a yelp and Alix plunged through the glass and sprawled on to the gravel in front of him. Theo stepped back in alarm. The doors were still closed; it looked as though Alix had been thrown through.

The next instant a man stepped through the closed doors and grabbed Alix. He was a great brawny thug, with short clipped grizzled grey hair and a scar across his cheek. He looked as if he had once been a boxer. Theo immediately recognized him from the planning meeting. It was Drake. He picked up Alix and, holding her above his head, staggered towards the lake.

Theo looked on in horror. Trying to pull himself together, he followed. He must do something. He must try and save Alix.

Theo hurled himself at Drake and tried to drag back his arms so as to free Alix. But it was as if he was clutching at cobwebs. He was powerless against the ghost. He watched helplessly as Drake swung Alix about and then tossed her far out into the lake. There was a small splash and Alix disappeared beneath the water.

The ghost turned to face Theo.

"I'll do for you, you varmint," growled Drake, as he stepped forwards, his arms out and his great hands like grappling hooks.

He's a ghost, thought Theo, surely he can't actually *do* anything – he can't throw *me* into the lake? But he couldn't help stepping back as Drake came towards him. The man looked so menacing.

The next moment Drake was on to him. Ghostly arms encircled Theo and although he felt nothing holding him, the chill was so great that suddenly he couldn't breathe. Theo struggled to free himself but every step he took, Drake followed like a shadow. Far worse than a shadow, it was as if Theo was completely enveloped in an icy shroud.

Theo began to panic. How was the man doing this? Was this was why the Jellicons didn't bother with alarm systems? They didn't need them with Drake at the house? Was this what his grandma had meant about the ghost being dangerous?

Theo felt so cold he was sure he would end as a block of ice. He ran towards the house but still Drake followed. He was getting weaker. There seemed nothing he could do against the phantom. As he gasped for air his breath seemed to freeze in front of him.

Theo forced himself to cry out, "Get off! Get off!"

He felt suddenly tired. All he wanted to do was sleep. He could feel his eyelids getting heavy and his strength gradually slipping away. But a dim shape appeared before his drowsy eyes, a shape he seemed to recognize, a shape that meant help was near. Theo knew he must struggle. He must not give up.

There was a sudden movement and the chill around Theo's body wavered. He saw Drake momentarily stare ahead before his expression went blank and he slumped to the ground. Theo fell on to his knees, gasping down great gulps of air.

"Hmm," said a voice. "Lucky I came along."

Theo looked up and there was Wat, triumphantly

holding up what looked like a huge twiggy toilet brush.

"Wat!" gasped Theo, the warm air burning his throat. His body was still chilled to the bone. "How did you get here?"

"I walked," said Wat. "I knew something was up when I saw Alix pinch the coach. And Mrs Cringle wanted me to give Drake a taste of tickler. So I thought I'd kill two birds with one stone, so to speak." The body of Drake stirred in front of him and Wat landed another whacking blow on the man's head. He sunk forwards and lay still. Then Wat put down his stick and rummaged in his apron pocket. He took out the handcuffs.

"Been wanting to use these for a while," said Wat. He pulled the unconscious Drake's arms back behind him and fastened the cuffs around his wrists. "Now then, we'd better put him somewhere out of the way." Wat looked round. "Ah, that'll do."

There was a stone trough with an old hand pump nearby, presumably left from the previous house and now made into a garden feature. Wat dragged Drake towards the trough and dumped him in it. It was full of water.

"Should be all right there for a bit," he said. "Now then, where's Alix?"

"He threw her in the lake," said Theo, looking anxiously towards the stretch of water. It was still and silent, without the slightest ripple.

Wat and Theo ran to the edge and looked in. The water was dark and murky. As the moon came from behind a cloud and shone full on the garden, Theo scanned the surface of the lake for any sign of Alix. There was nothing, not even the slightest hint. Alix had gone.

# 15

Theo and Wat rushed along the edge of the lake, peering into the water. All Theo could see in the moonlight was his own faint reflection.

A bit further round, the lake narrowed and there was an arched bridge joining the two banks. They ran over to it to see if they could get a better view and leant over the rail, gazing into the water.

Still nothing. Alix seemed to have disappeared without trace. Then, just as they were about to give up, a ripple caught Theo's eye and he saw the faintest smudge of pink.

"There!" cried Theo, pointing.

"Hmm," grunted Wat.

"Quickly," said Theo.

They ran off the bridge and waded into the water.

Alix was floating just below the surface.

As they pulled her out, Theo was struck at how light and cold she was. It didn't feel as if she was remotely alive. They laid her down on the grassy bank, the water running off her.

Theo looked at Wat. He said nothing.

Theo wasn't sure what to do. What was it like for a not-really-dead person to drown? *Could* they drown? Alix didn't appear to be breathing but then Theo couldn't remember whether she usually did so or not. It wasn't the sort of thing you noticed in people.

Theo had once done a first aid course at school. He'd learnt how to do artificial resuscitation. He thought hard, trying to remember the procedure. He knew that to start off with you had to make sure that there was nothing in the person's mouth. Theo knelt down by Alix and looked closely at her.

Alix's body gave a sudden jerk, and she coughed violently. Muddy water sprayed straight into Theo's face.

"What are you doing, you berk?"

"You're all right?" spluttered Theo.

"Of course I'm all right," said Alix. She struggled to her feet, and stood there shakily.

"We thought you were. . ." began Wat, but his voice trailed off.

"Yeah, well I wasn't," said Alix. "I'm just wet. What happened to that spook?"

"Wat settled him," said Theo, busy wiping his face with his handkerchief.

"Well, let's get on with it then."

Alix marched off towards the house. Theo stared after her for a moment. He glanced at Wat, then they shrugged at each other and followed.

Without Drake to stop them it wasn't too difficult to get into the house. Alix managed to unlock the French doors and they stepped inside. Now Wat was with them, Theo was especially cautious for a moment or two in case the alarm went off. But it didn't. They started to search the house.

Wat, who couldn't read and so couldn't help with the search, sat down by the front door to keep watch in case the Jellicons returned.

Theo and Alix began with the study. They looked everywhere for a safe – the most obvious place to hide things – but couldn't find one anywhere. Otherwise, the only bit of furniture that might hide anything was the desk. The drawers held nothing apart from some stationery and a couple of paperclips. On the top were a few newspapers and magazines including *Golfing Monthly* and *Tycoon*.

"I'm going to look around upstairs," said Alix.

Theo sunk into a large padded armchair beside the fireplace. The grate was full of ash, as if someone had recently lit a fire. This seemed odd to Theo, as the weather hadn't been cold. His gaze wandered along bookshelves. They appeared to be there because they looked nice, rather than to be read; they all had fancy bindings and were neatly arranged. Then an idea struck Theo. Perhaps they were false books, with just backs and no pages, and they hid a secret door to the safe. He tugged a few of the spines to see but they were all real books.

Theo looked at the titles. There were some odd ones. He couldn't believe Jellicon was really interested in any of them. Who'd want to read a book called *A Complete History of Tiddlywinks*? Or *My Life as a Bus Conductor*? Surely not Jellicon. There was even a book called *Aluminium Production*.

Theo pulled the aluminium book off the shelf and opened it. It looked quite an interesting book. There was a nice map of Jamaica opposite the title page. Theo studied it for a few moments before hurriedly closing it. What was he thinking of? He couldn't sit reading Jellicon's books!

Theo carefully put the book back in its place. As he did so he happened to notice the dust. The whole shelf – in fact *all* the shelves – were covered in a thin layer of dust. Theo was surprised. Mr Windrush would like to see this, he thought. Just imagine the stories this dust would tell!

Theo smiled, thinking of Mr Windrush and his dust collection. But then it struck him that the dust in front of him was telling a story for *him*. As he'd taken the aluminium book off the shelf it had left tracks in the dust – nothing surprising in that – but Theo saw that there was only one other book on the shelves which had the same telltale marks beside it. Since the dust had settled, Mr Jellicon had only touched one book, a thick one called *The Bookkeeper's Companion*.

Theo took the book off the shelf. The moment he did so he realized that it wasn't a real book. It had been made to look like a book from outside but it was actually a box. With increasing excitement, Theo put it down on the desk and opened the lid.

It was a box file – inside was a spring clip for keeping papers tidy – and it held a few bits of paper. Theo pulled back the clip and looked at them.

To his immense disappointment, they were just bills for work that Mr Jellicon had had done. There was one from Randalls for shoe repair. Another was from Shane Builders for drainage works. And the third was from a firm called Muldoon & Holmes. The heading didn't say any more about their business but when Theo saw the bill, his heart missed a beat. It was for "tracking down and acquiring all 200 copies of the privately printed book *The Cringle Bequest*".

Theo could hardly believe it. So that was it! Jellicon had got hold of every single copy of the book about the tower. And he'd probably destroyed them, too, thought Theo. Perhaps that was what the ashes were in the fire – all that was left of the Reverend Algernon Brusset's books.

Suddenly Theo understood the importance of the piece of paper in his hand. It was the evidence they needed. It would show that Jellicon had been behaving dishonestly. He must hang on to it at all costs.

"What the deuce do you think you're doing?" said a voice from the doorway.

Theo looked up. His spirits plummeted. It was Josiah Jellicon.

# 16

If you are going to do something and you don't want to get caught, it's a good idea to make sure of your escape route before anything else. That way, you're less likely to find yourself in an awkward situation that you can't do anything about. And another thing: if you have someone acting as lookout, it helps if they are reliable.

Theo knew immediately that he was trapped. There was no way out of the study except through the doorway and Josiah Jellicon was standing in the middle of that.

It was easy to see what had happened. The study was at the back of the house which was why he hadn't heard the car return. The Bentley hardly roared anyway. But what had happened to Wat? Why hadn't he warned them?

These thoughts flashed through Theo's mind as he stood there, looking at Mr Jellicon.

"I might have known you'd turn up here, snooping around," growled Jellicon. "I should have guessed when I saw you at the planning meeting, sticking your nose into things that don't concern you. Well, you'll not get away with it this time. The police will be here in a minute. Yes, I knew we had an intruder. The alarm system doesn't ring any bells, just alerts me discreetly via my mobile. It took me a lot of effort to organize this golf club scheme and I'm not going to allow a flea like you to ruin everything. So you can give me that."

Theo was still holding the bill from Muldoon & Holmes. Jellicon stepped forwards, away from the door, holding out his hand. What was he to do now? thought Theo. He'd be in big trouble when the police turned up, but if he could keep hold of the bill he'd have the proof he needed.

A movement behind Jellicon caught his eye. Alix had stepped into the room. Jellicon saw Theo's glance and turned, and at that moment Theo acted. He dashed forward holding the paper out towards Alix.

"Take it!" he cried. "Run!"

"What the –?" exclaimed Jellicon, staring open-mouthed. He hadn't the slightest idea what was happening. All he could see was the piece of paper, seemingly floating away in mid-air.

Clutching the bill, Alix ran for the front door, which was open wide.

"Oh no you don't!" cried Mrs Jellicon, who had just entered the hallway. She stood in front of the door-way, barring the exit.

Alix seemed surprised to see Mrs Jellicon. She skidded to a stop and appeared unsure what to do.

"Go on, Alix!" urged Theo.

"You think you're so clever, don't you?" sneered Mrs Jellicon, moving towards Alix, like a leopard about to spring. "You and your ghostly friends. I suppose that brute asleep on the steps did for Drake? Well you've not won yet. You should have known you'd meet your match here."

"Lola, what are you saying? What's going on?" Mr Jellicon scratched his head. He hadn't the faintest idea what all this was about.

Standing behind him, Theo saw his chance. He dodged out and, arms outstretched, flung himself at Mrs Jellicon.

"Aah!" she cried, as she fell over and Theo tumbled on top of her.

"Hey!" bawled Jellicon. "You ruffian!"

"Run Alix! Don't let them get it!" shouted Theo, as Jellicon grabbed him.

Alix at last came to her senses. Gripping the piece of paper tightly, she dashed out of the door and into the driveway.

"I suppose that's Muldoon's bill she's got?" said Mrs Jellicon, struggling quickly to her feet.

"She?" said Jellicon, who had a tight grip on Theo.

"Oh, never mind. She's getting away. You'd better bring him. Hurry."

Theo was hauled roughly out of the house. Twisting round, he was just in time to see Alix disappear into a dense group of trees at the side of the driveway. Mrs Jellicon set off after her but her heels sank into the lawn.

"Argh!" she cried, kicking off her shoes.

A moment later the phantom horses sprang from the trees pulling the coach behind them. Alix was on top, holding the reins. They tore down the drive towards the gates.

"Curses!" cried Mrs Jellicon, waving her fists. "She's got transport. Quickly Josiah, into the car. She's getting away!"

Mr Jellicon, still completely bemused, pushed Theo into the back of the Bentley.

"Lola! My sweet, what on earth is going on?" he exclaimed as he got into the front passenger seat. Mrs Jellicon started the engine.

"Just keep an eye on him," she shouted. "And make sure he doesn't try anything." Theo, peeping out of the car from the back seat, saw the phantom coach disappear through the gates at the end of the drive. Mrs Jellicon slammed her foot on the accelerator and the car lurched forwards, throwing Theo backwards. They shot off down the drive after the phantom coach.

"Lola, will you please –" began Jellicon, then he stared ahead and his mouth dropped open in horror. "*LOOK OUT!*" he bawled.

The speeding car was almost at the end of the driveway . . . and the heavy steel gates were still closed.

# 17

Mrs Jellicon slammed on the brakes and the car skidded on the gravel.

"Oh, come on!" she muttered as the gates swung slowly open. She revved the engine and, as soon as she could, drove out into the lane.

There was no sign of the phantom coach. Mrs Jellicon put her foot down on the accelerator.

As they sped down the country lane, Theo couldn't help being impressed at the way the car held the road. In the front seat Josiah Jellicon was becoming more and more alarmed.

"Will . . . will you please tell me what's going on?" he gibbered.

"The girl has got the bill, hasn't she?" yelled Mrs Jellicon at her husband.

"Bill, yes. But what girl? Where?" Jellicon shouted back at her, staring about. "I can't see anybody. Why are we in such a rush?"

"I can't explain now!"

"Can't you go a little slower?" mumbled Jellicon. "This car . . . it was very expensive. . ."

They sped around a corner and there was the phantom coach, tearing along ahead of them.

"Phew," murmured Mrs Jellicon, keeping her foot down. The car crept closer.

Suddenly the headlights of an oncoming car with a blue flashing light shone straight at them and Mrs Jellicon swerved to the side of the road.

"Oh, and about time!" she muttered.

The Bentley rode up the verge as the police car passed and then it settled back on to the road. Theo looked out of the back window. The police car disappeared around the corner, its siren blaring.

In front, the phantom coach had also disappeared.

"Drat! Now where have they gone?" cried Mrs Jellicon and she put her foot down further.

They dashed through a village and then, after few more twists and turns in the road, they could see the phantom coach again, going at the most terrific speed. Theo, glancing at the speedo, was surprised to see that the Bentley was going at nearly 95 miles per hour. In that case, what was Alix doing? He had to admire the way she was handling the horses.

"Thank goodness," said Mrs Jellicon. "Now we'll catch them." She edged the car faster and nearer.

Mr Jellicon clutched the armrest on the side of the door, digging his fingernails into the soft leather upholstery.

"I still fail to see –" he began but then he turned away, shutting his eyes tightly as another car came towards them. Mrs Jellicon swerved slightly. And then they were going down the hill into Bunting.

The long steep hill had a few twists and turns. Anybody who was looking would wonder what on earth the people in the Bentley were doing driving at such a rate, but of course they wouldn't have seen the phantom coach, its foaming horses seemingly flying through the air.

The car reached the last straight run down into the town and Theo's stomach lurched as he realized that the hill ended in a junction. They'd have to turn sharp right or left if they were going to avoid the car sales showroom straight ahead, its cars polished and gleaming, and enhanced by a huge mirror on the back wall.

"*Noooo!*" wailed Jellicon as his wife continued to drive at tremendous speed after, or so it appeared to him, nothing-at-all. Theo watched as the phantom coach headed straight for the showroom window. It wasn't going to stop. He suddenly understood what Alix was doing. He saw the great sheet of glass appear to wobble as the horses and the coach went through. Then the mirror also shuddered and closed after them like a curtain. They disappeared.

"No! No! No!" exclaimed Mrs Jellicon. She hauled round the steering wheel as hard as she could. The Bentley spun round, skidded sideways across the road and bumped up the pavement, stopping inches from the plate glass window.

"Aarggghhhhh!" shouted Mrs Jellicon. "They've got away!"

Mr Jellicon was breathing heavily. "I can't believe you've just done that!"

A few seconds later, a small piece of paper fluttered down through the air. It settled on the windscreen and stayed there just long enough for Theo to see what it was, then it slipped off on to the ground.

"Incredible!" cried Mrs Jellicon. She hurried to open the car door but the car was too close to the showroom window and that way out was blocked.

"Quick! Get out! Get out!" she cried, shooing her husband out of his side.

"Whatever now?" mumbled Jellicon, who got out and stood, still shaking after the drive.

"Where is it? Where is it?" muttered Mrs Jellicon, who was scrabbling under the car. "Ah! Quickly! There it goes!"

Theo watched from the back seat, as Mrs Jellicon chased after the bit of paper as it was carried away by the breeze. Her husband stumbled after her.

"Yes. Yes. Yes!" she cried, leaping up and grasping the paper. "I've got it!" Triumphant, she stood looking at the bill for a moment. "This is what you should have done ages ago!"

Mrs Jellicon screwed the piece of paper into a ball, stuffed it into her mouth and swallowed.

"But . . . but. . ." cried Jellicon, aghast. "I haven't paid that!"

Theo saw his chance. He pushed forward the passenger seat and slipped out of the doorway. Using the Bentley as cover, he crept away and the moment he was round the corner he started to run.

Well, that's that, thought Theo. After running for a few blocks he slowed his pace to a walk. It seemed unlikely that the Jellicons would come after him.

What had happened? Why had Alix dropped the document at the last minute? He couldn't make it out. What was certain was that now it really was all over. The bill from Muldoon & Holmes had been the only bit of evidence against Jellicon and they'd lost it. Theo felt cheated. They'd been so close. It just wasn't fair.

His way home led past the library. As he was walking down the path beside the building he happened to glance in through a window. He caught sight of a slight bluish glow and stopped to look.

The room was a small one off the main part of the library and housed the photocopier. At a desk in the corner there sat a man. He was reading from a book and making notes on a piece of paper. The man was a ghost.

Theo tried to remember the family photos. He was almost sure it was his grandfather. He tapped on the glass to try and attract his attention. He wanted to tell his grandfather that he'd tried to get hold of the book but that it was missing, and that he thought Jellicon had got hold of it and destroyed it. But although Theo tapped loudly, the man seemed not to hear. He went on reading as if he was in another world.

After a while Theo gave up trying to attract the man's attention and continued sadly along the road.

The quickest way home was through the cemetery.

Not many people would choose to walk through a cemetery late at night. Even Theo, who was getting used to seeing ghosts around, would not normally have done it. But he was keen to get home. He was tired and wanted to go to bed. So he hurried in through the gate.

About halfway along the path, he glimpsed a figure he recognized, standing beside a gravestone.

"Oh, no!" muttered Theo. "That's all I need!" He started running.

"Oh no you don't!" said Grandma, and she stuck out her stick as he dashed past.

Despite the fact that it was a ghost stick and shouldn't have made much impression on Theo, Grandma chose just the right moment. If applied at the right moment, even the tiniest force can have an impressive effect. Theo's right foot was off the ground when she struck it with her stick. It caught behind Theo's left leg as he ran and he fell sprawling on to the pavement.

"You little fool," said Grandma. "I told you to leave things alone. Don't you ever do what you're told? And you had to encourage this silly girl along too."

"I didn't!" protested Theo, struggling to his feet. He saw that Grandma's left hand had a firm grip on Alix's ear.

"Ow!" moaned Alix.

"She's the one that suggested it," said Theo. "It was her idea."

"Can't take the blame yourself, can you? You always were a whiny little maggot."

Theo rubbed his grazed knees.

"But Jellicon *was* up to something! We knew he was. We found the evidence."

"All right then, where is it?" demanded Grandma.

"Alix dropped it," said Theo.

"I didn't!" protested Alix. "It was the window. It didn't go through."

"Idiots!" cried Grandma. "You should have known that it wouldn't go through. It's not from Deadland. So I suppose Jellicon got it back?"

Theo nodded.

"Then what happened?"

"Mrs Jellicon ate it," said Theo, trying not to smile.

"He he!" giggled Alix. "I hope it gives her bellyache!"

"That's enough!" cried Grandma, giving Alix's ear a twist.

"Oww!" cried Alix.

"You're both hopeless little twerps," thundered Grandma. "I'm no fool, whatever you think. I told you to leave off for a very good reason. With Drake's appearance, I needed to find out what was happening. Now you've ruined everything. Alix, you'll stay in Deadland from now on. No more jolly jaunts for you! And Theo, go home – and for once, stay out of trouble."

Theo stood still. He was reluctant to set off home, at least not until he'd asked his grandma something.

"Grandma. . ." He wasn't sure how to start.

"What is it?" asked Grandma, sharply.

"At the library, just now. . ."

"What? Oh . . . yes, yes, it's your grandfather," said Grandma. "I don't suppose he noticed you. The world could end and he wouldn't notice. Always got his nose in a book. But he's a kind man. He never *does* anything, but he's kind."

She turned and started dragging Alix away.

"Ow!" cried Alix. "Let go!"

"Be quiet, you little tyke. You're coming with me. You've got some horses to muck out."

Theo watched as they disappeared into the gloom. Then he set off for home as fast as he could.

# 19

The next morning, which was Friday, Theo decided that he should retrieve his bicycle from outside the The Magnolias. After what had happened the previous night, he wasn't at all keen to go anywhere near the Jellicons' house but he thought putting off the trip would probably only lead to more trouble. If his bike was discovered then he'd have to explain why it was there and he didn't fancy doing that.

As he was walking through the town he met the librarian, Miss Sheldon, on her way to work.

"Oh, hello," she said. "I've been hoping you'd call at the library. I wanted to tell you I looked everywhere for your book but without success. I'm afraid it's gone for good."

"Never mind," said Theo, who wasn't surprised.

Muldoon & Holmes had been very thorough. "Thank you for looking. I appreciate it."

When Theo reached The Magnolias about an hour and a half later, he was relieved to see that his bicycle was still hidden in the bushes.

He kept a sharp eye out for the Jellicons. The last thing he wanted to do was bump into them. Theo thought that they might let matters rest, now the evidence against them had been destroyed, but he didn't want to take any chances.

Just as he was pulling his bicycle from its hiding place he heard the gates begin to open and he backed quickly behind the foliage. A moment later the Jellicons sailed past in the red Bentley. Theo waited for a few moments to make quite sure that they were well on their way, then he set off for home.

It was a sunny day and as Theo neared Bunting he decided to take a short detour and cycle past Cringle's Tower. It was some time since he'd last seen it close to. In fact, he'd never paid it much attention before getting involved with Jellicon's plans.

A barbed wire fence had been put up all around with several large KEEP OUT signs in red letters. Getting off his bicycle, Theo leant it against a fence post and climbed through. He wanted to have a closer look.

The tower looked a bit like a lighthouse. At the top there was a room with windows all round which Theo supposed was where Mrs Cringle had watched for her husband's ship. An outside staircase, built of stone with a metal balustrade, led to a door about halfway up. The tower was covered in creepers and its base was thick with brambles.

With great difficulty, and getting badly scratched, Theo struggled through the brambles and reached the bottom step of the staircase. The stone was worn and crumbling and the rail rusty. Treading carefully, he went up the steps and reached the door which was secured with a large padlock. The door itself looked sound but the frame was rotten. He tried pushing the door and immediately the hasp that held the padlock fell away and the door swung open with a loud creak.

It was dark and dusty inside but there was just enough light from the open door for Theo to see a second staircase, leading to the room at the top. Otherwise the tower was empty.

Theo was just about to try the second staircase when a movement by the door caught his eye. A figure stood in the doorway. To his horror he saw that it was the ghost of the butler, Drake.

"What?" growled Drake. "YOU!"

As the ghost stepped towards him, Theo started to back away up the stairs. What was the ghost doing here? Had he followed all the way from The Magnolias? Theo didn't stop to ask. After three steps he turned and ran as fast as he could to the top where he dashed into the observation room. He slammed the door shut and leant against it, gasping for breath.

A second later Theo felt an icy chill pierce his body like a knife. He gasped with shock and fell forward, sprawling on the floor.

What Theo had forgotten in his rush to escape, was that it's no good closing a door on a ghost. You can lock it and bolt it but it still won't do any good. The ghost just walks straight through. That's what Drake had done, and he'd walked through Theo's body at the same time.

Chilled to the bone, Theo rolled on the floor, trying to get away from Drake. But then he reached the wall and could go no further.

Drake looked down and grinned at him with a grin like the jagged edge of a rusty can. He knew Theo was trapped. He could take his time.

"I'll teach you to play tricks! You'll not meddle with me again, when I've finished with you," he roared.

But before Drake could take another step, there was a piercing whistle and through the glass windows of the observation room flew dozens of black crows. Squawking furiously, they descended on Drake.

"Aah! Get off!" cried Drake, as the birds started to peck him. He threw his fists around trying to knock the birds away but they were too quick for him. "Get off! Get off! Aaaargh!"

Blinded by the whirling mass of birds, he stumbled about the room. Finally he reached the wall and, passing through, tumbled out of the tower.

Theo pulled himself to his feet and staggered to the window. He caught a glimpse of the birds, looking like a small black cloud, before they disappeared over the cliff.

"Well, wasn't it lucky I was here?"

It was Alix.

"Alix!" cried Theo, turning round. "How come?"

"I wanted to get my own back on that bully," said Alix. "Sent him a message saying if he came here he'd learn something. Heh, that'll teach him!"

"I thought you weren't supposed to leave Deadland?" said Theo.

"Yeah, well I did. Not going to let a small matter like your grandma stop me when I have important things to do." Alix sniffed. Theo wondered what punishment Grandma would inflict.

Theo thought about how his grandma had so much say in what went on in Deadland. How had she managed to take over like that, organizing everybody? He supposed it was because she liked doing things. She always had; she was just one of those people. That must be why she was involved with the outfit called LIMBO.

"Thanks Alix, you're a pal," said Theo. "I would've been in real trouble without you."

"Don't mention it," said Alix, looking out of the window.

Theo looked at the not-really-dead girl for a moment. There was something he'd been wanting to ask for some time.

"Alix?" he said.

"Yeah?"

"How did you get to Deadland, Alix?"

Alix didn't speak for a minute. She seemed to have become edgy. "I'm not saying."

"Go on!"

"No, I don't want to."

"Why not, Alix?"

"Because I don't *know*, that's why!" shouted Alix, and she stomped across the room, through the door and was gone.

"Alix!" cried Theo. "Alix, wait! Wait!"

Theo ran after her. He tried to open the door to follow but the door wouldn't budge. He tugged at the handle with all his strength but it made no difference. It was stuck fast.

"Oh, blast!" cried Theo, hammering his fists on the door in frustration.

He was stuck at the top of Cringle's Tower.

And in a few days' time, it was going to be demolished.

Theo thought about what to do. If he couldn't open the door, there was only one way out – through one of the windows. He looked to see if he could open one. The tower was covered in creepers and he might be able to climb down. He went right round the whole room trying every window. But they were all stuck fast.

"Help!" shouted Theo, but he realized shouting was pointless. No one would hear him. How could they, with the windows closed tight? And anyway, he couldn't see anybody outside.

He tried not to think of what might happen if nobody checked the room before demolishing the tower. But surely the demolition company would look? Surely that was standard procedure?

Theo didn't want to wait to find out. With Jellicon, anything was possible. The only option was to try and break open a window. Someone was bound to turn up sooner or later. Then he'd be able to shout and attract their attention.

Theo chose what he thought was the weakest window. There was a gap at the bottom which let in a draught and part of the frame felt soft and rotten. He stood back. He'd have to judge it just right. He didn't want to fall out.

He charged at the window and knocked it with his shoulder, throwing his weight into it.

Nothing happened.

He tried again, standing a little further back.

Still nothing happened.

He stood at the far side of the room, took a deep breath and charged again.

There was a crunch as Theo hit the window frame. He saw the whole window burst outwards and hang momentarily in the air before beginning to fall. The next instant Theo was following, tumbling out over the sill. He tried desperately to grab the edge of the frame but missed it. Frantically he clutched at anything that was within reach, anything to stop himself falling. At last his hands tightened around a bit of creeper and he held on with all his strength. Somersaulting through the air, he hit the outside wall with a "thwack" that drove the breath from his body.

"Ooof!" cried Theo.

When he recovered a little, he took a careful look down.

"Oh, custard!" he muttered.

He was high up on the outside of the tower. The creepers directly below him gave a little support to his feet but didn't look as though they'd take his full weight. He daren't let go with his hands in case the branches didn't hold him. There didn't seem to be any way he could climb down. He had no choice but to hold on until he was rescued. He tried not to think about the brambles at the bottom of the tower.

The minutes passed. After what seemed like an age, he was relieved to see a car drive up. A man and a woman got out with a small boy. The boy ran towards the tower, stopping at the fence. The man started taking photographs.

"Mommy, look!" shouted the little boy.

The man and the woman looked up at the tower and at Theo.

Theo was about to speak when the creepers started to give way beneath his feet.

"Aargh!" he cried, almost losing his grip.

He slipped down a little but then his shirt caught on a branch and stopped him falling further. He tried not to look at the brambles.

"Is this the tower thing that they're going to demolish?" asked the woman.

Theo nodded. He tried to speak. He wanted to say that he needed rescuing but no words came out. His shirt was too tight around his chest.

"Are you a protester?" asked the woman. "Honey, look, there's a protester. This is the tower, all right."

"*Ccca yuhh –*" gasped Theo.

"Oh isn't that wonderful!" said the man. "You are so brave, staying there when they're going to blow the whole thing up. I do admire you protesters."

"Cute tower," said the woman. "Shame they're going to knock it down. Honey, will you take a picture?"

The woman stood with the little boy in front of the tower while the man took a photograph.

"Hey, could you move a little more to the left?" the man called to Theo. "OK, I guess not."

"*Whhhh aaa,*" said Theo.

"Hey, honey, those people in the hotel would really like to see this," said the woman.

"Why, I hadn't thought of that! I'll call them!" The man took out a mobile phone.

"*Rrrrrrrrrr*," said Theo.

"You just stay there, honey, you're doing a great job," said the woman.

Ten minutes later, two more cars drove up and parked next to the first one.

People got out. They moved about and took photographs, talking excitedly about the tower being demolished and pointing at Theo.

"*Cccccca suuuu*," tried Theo. But nobody took any notice.

After Theo had been stuck in the creeper on the tower for about half an hour a reporter and photographer turned up.

"What's your name, please? And you're dead against this tower being demolished?" asked the reporter.

Theo shook his head. "*Ccc!*"

Next a large van arrived with "TV – Outside Broadcast" written on it. The crew jumped out clutching cameras and sound equipment and a woman with blonde hair immediately started talking to the camera.

"The latest in the saga of Cringle's Tower. Local protest has been muted until now but here at the tower one young man has taken it upon himself to thwart the demolition experts."

At that moment, Theo felt the creeper shift slightly. His shirt began to loosen and, regaining his voice at last, he just managed to shout out "*Heelllpppp!*" as the creeper tore away from the crumbling wall. It fell forwards quite slowly, pitching Theo into the middle of the bramble bush at the bottom of the tower.

## 21

"We saw you on television!" cried Ruth, excitedly.

Ruth, aged five, was one of Theo's fourteen sisters. They'd all come with Theo's mum and dad to collect him from hospital. Theo's descent into the brambles had not done any serious damage but the doctors had spent several hours doing tests to make sure. Finally they'd looked at his tongue, checked his pulse and said that he could go home.

Theo's fall had been captured by the television crew and transmitted on the six o'clock news. There was also film of his rescue from the thorns by a couple of courageous paramedics, who carried him on a stretcher to the waiting ambulance.

Theo's sisters had taped the whole thing so that he could watch it when he got home. Theo was rather thrilled that they thought he was some kind of hero.

"You're famous!" cried Stella.

"You were very brave," said Ruth.

"What *were* you doing?" asked Theo's mum.

"You could have been seriously hurt!" said his dad.

"He was protesting, Mum. That's what it said on the news," said Anne.

"Protesting about what?" said Mrs Slugg.

"The tower, of course. They're going to knock it down and build a golf course."

"But why? The plans were passed on Wednesday, weren't they?"

The news report showed Theo being carried off in the ambulance.

The presenter turned to Mr Jellicon.

"Of course, I'm deeply sorry that a protester has been hurt," said Jellicon, smirking slightly. "But the demolition will go ahead as planned. And I'd like to point out that the new golf club and restaurant will be open to everyone, subject to the usual conditions."

Then there was an advertisement for Jellicon Comestibles.

"I can't understand why you did it," said Mrs Slugg.

"You were foolish to even think of it, if you ask me," said Mr Slugg. "It's not as if Mr Jellicon hasn't done everything above board. He's gone to the proper authorities."

Theo decided that it was simplest not to say what had really happened.

His mother insisted that he spend the night inside the flat so she could make quite sure he was all right. Theo was rather relieved by this because he thought that that way he would perhaps avoid Grandma. When she heard the news, she was bound to have something to say about the matter. But he had no such luck.

"Silly little sprat," she said, sitting down in the armchair a few moments after Theo's mum had left him to go to sleep. "Fancy getting caught in a bramble bush."

"I didn't know the creeper was going to give way," hissed Theo.

"What were you doing there, anyway?"

Theo didn't say anything. If his Grandma didn't know, he wasn't going to tell her about Alix and Drake. Perhaps Alix had got back without her noticing. He hoped so.

"Go away, Grandma, please."

"Suppose you thought you could stop the demolition? Well of all the stupid ideas. . . How can I organize anything if you don't do what you're told? I told you to leave off and stay out of trouble. And what do you do? You go and climb up the blooming tower. Then what – and it couldn't get much worse – you're all over the six o'clock news! Theo Slugg, you're a witless worm and no grandson of mine!"

"I wish that was true," muttered Theo to himself.

At least he'd tried, he thought. Although he hadn't intended to protest like that, it might have worked. Then what would his Grandma have said? Nothing, probably. There was no pleasing her.

He groaned softly as if in pain and, closing his eyes, turned over.

Grandma went on grumbling but Theo ignored her, and eventually she gave up and went away. In a few minutes he was asleep.

# 22

On Monday, Theo nearly didn't go to watch the demolition.

"Aren't you going?" asked Mrs Slugg. "What, not after your protest?"

"He wanted to save it, Mum," said Kate. "Not to see it fall down."

"That's it," said Mr Slugg, who was getting ready for work. "It will be too upsetting."

"No, I'm going to go," said Theo, though he didn't really know why. It would hardly be fun watching Jellicon's triumph.

"Perhaps you'll be on the news again," said Ruth.

Theo got ready to go out. When the lift reached the ground floor, he found Mr Windrush was waiting. He had a large cardboard box full of jam jars. They were from his dust collection.

"What a lot of dust, Mr Windrush," said Theo.

"Yes, I'm going to store it in the basement. I need the shelf space for my more recent sweepings."

All the jars had labels. One of them caught Theo's eye.

"Mr Windrush, is that dust from the library?" he asked.

"Yes, that's right," said Mr Windrush, picking up the jar. "I collected that a long time ago, before the reorganization."

"So it's from books that have gone missing, is it?"

"No, why?" asked Mr Windrush, looking puzzled.

"The label says 'Public Library: GM'. That means 'Gone Missing', doesn't it?" said Theo.

"No, no. Oh dear me, no," said Mr Windrush, looking taken aback. "That means 'General Manuscripts'. It's a big box of writing by local authors. There are no bound books, just hand-written sheets."

Theo stood staring at Mr Windrush. It took a moment for what he'd said to sink in.

"Blimey!" he cried. "Excuse me, Mr Windrush, I've got to run."

* * *

Ten minutes later, Theo reached the library and dashed in through the door. He looked around for the librarian, Miss Sheldon. She was nowhere to be seen. Instead there was a man at the desk. Theo went up to him.

"Is Miss Sheldon here?" he asked, trying to catch his breath.

"No, sorry," said the man. "She's taken the day off. I think she may be going to watch the demolition of the tower."

"Oh, no!" groaned Theo.

This was too much to bear. What was he to do now?

Then Theo remembered Nigel, who knew the librarian. Perhaps he would be able to help.

Theo ran into Luigi's Café and slumped into a chair.

"Mr Theo is not looking happy today," said Nigel, coming over.

"Nigel," gasped Theo. "You've got to help."

Nigel sat down. "Tell me, my friend."

"It's the tower," panted Theo. "I need to contact the librarian."

"Miss Sheldon?" asked Nigel.

Theo nodded. "It's really urgent."

"Then tell me the message, my friend, and I will help you."

"You can?"

"Yes," said Nigel, looking serious. "No problem."

"I'll write it down," said Theo, and on a scrap of paper he wrote: 'GM = General Manuscripts'.

There's a saying that all publicity is good publicity. The idea is that it is much better that something is talked about, even if everything people are saying is bad, than that it is not talked about at all.

If it hadn't been for Theo's supposed protest then probably there would have been hardly anybody to watch the demolition of Cringle's Tower. But when Theo arrived there later that morning, a large crowd had gathered.

During the days following his descent into the brambles there were several items on the local television news. Several people called at Vanilla Villas to interview Theo, including a lady from the *New York Times*. It seemed that at last the sleepy town of Bunting had woken up to the fact that it was about to lose one of its most cherished treasures. The truth, of course, was that everybody liked to have an opinion about anything that made it into the news and before

Theo's celebrity, nobody had paid much attention to Jellicon's plans. A local historian was dug out from beneath his books to give his opinion. He used words such as "disgrace" and "monument" and everybody nodded agreement. It looked as though Jellicon would have to reconsider. And then Jellicon appeared, all smiles, and charmed people with his plans. Everybody changed their views and wondered why they'd put up with such a decaying wreck of a building for so long.

Theo stayed out of it all, as far as he could. He thought he'd done his bit. And anyway, whatever anybody said on television, it seemed certain that Jellicon would get his way and the demolition would go ahead as planned.

Jellicon had called in the Acme Demolition Company to do the actual demolition. The television news showed them arranging their equipment and the project manager was interviewed about "controlled explosions", "exclusion zones" and "non-electric detonators".

"Everybody please keep outside the exclusion zone," he said sternly, now talking on a loudspeaker system. He was wearing a hard hat and a luminous jacket.

The tower was surrounded by barriers and bits of red and white stripy tape. This was the exclusion zone.

"There will be a two minute warning. A siren will sound. Please be sure you are behind the barriers."

The Jellicons arrived in the red Bentley. They parked the car a safe distance away and walked towards a platform where the microphones and loud-speakers were set up. Mrs Jellicon was going to push the button that set off the explosives. They climbed on to the platform. The television crew were filming everything.

The project manager explained how the demolition was going to work and then Mr Jellicon stepped up to the microphone. He took a piece of paper from his pocket.

"Ladies and gentlemen, friends and colleagues, neighbours and visitors. We are gathered here today to witness the start of the future. This development heralds a new beginning for our town of Bunting. Generations from now, your grandchildren's grand-children will look back on this day as one of great significance, a new start for the community. It now gives me great pleasure to hand over to my dear wife, who has agreed to press the button."

Mrs Jellicon, wearing a cream suit and a large straw hat, stepped forward.

She smiled at everybody.

"Just press the button," said the project manager.

The siren sounded.

"Everybody please remain behind the barriers."

Mrs Jellicon gave the button a terrific whack with her fist. There was a loud BOOM! and a tremendous cloud of dust obscured the tower. Everybody watched excitedly as the cloud gradually cleared away.

There was a sigh from the crowd. The tower was still standing.

The project manager, looking decidedly flustered, hurried up to the microphone. "Please remain behind the barriers. The tower is extremely unsafe." It was obvious to Theo that something had gone wrong and the project manager wasn't quite sure what to do next.

At that moment a car drove up and pulled up beside the Bentley. Two people got out, a man and a woman. To Theo's surprise he recognized them. It was the librarian and the planning officer.

"Thank goodness!" cried the planning officer. "We thought we'd be too late. Miss Sheldon has found something extraordinary. Ah, there you are, young man. Step forward! You were right! You were right all along!"

"I found it!" said the librarian. "It was in a box in the store. I'd never have thought to look there. But you were right! If it hadn't have been for you we would never have known."

"What? What?" cried the television crew, turning their cameras towards the new arrivals.

Jellicon looked furious. Mrs Jellicon's face matched her dress.

"The tower belongs to the people of Bunting," announced the planning officer. "It shouldn't be demolished. In fact the owner of the land is obliged to maintain it, granting access to the public at all times. It's all here, in a document enclosed with this manuscript that Miss Sheldon has found. I'm so pleased that we weren't too late."

Josiah Jellicon had gone grey. He staggered slightly and clutched the rail of the platform for support. On his face was a curious half-smile.

At that moment there was a strange rumble from the tower. It got louder and louder and then with a great roar and another huge cloud of dust, Cringle's Tower collapsed into a heap of rubble.

# 23

After the demolition of Cringle's Tower, Theo heard no more from Grandma or any of the other ghosts. He was a little surprised at this but also rather relieved. At least he could get on with doing his own things. He even got his project on aluminium done in time for the start of the school term.

Some weeks later, Mrs Trillaby and her dog got into the lift. There was nothing unusual in that, of course, as she took Pixie out for a walk every morning and evening. But on this occasion she poked her head around Theo's curtain.

"Hello, Theo," she said. Pixie started to sniff Theo's trainers.

"Hello, Mrs Trillaby," said Theo, looking up from his book. He was making a study of penguins – not for a school project but because his latest video game was set in Antarctica and involved a band of trained penguins sabotaging an environmental monitoring installation.

"Mr Windrush asked me to tell you not to forget your post," said Mrs Trillaby, touching her hair lightly with her right hand.

"Thank you, Mrs Trillaby, I'll go and collect it in a minute," said Theo, who hadn't forgotten about the post and wondered why Mr Windrush had mentioned it. "Oh, I do like the new hairstyle."

"Why, bless you," said Mrs Trillaby, beaming. "I was rather pleased with it. Julian has excelled himself, I think."

Mrs Trillaby's new hairdresser had created a series of swirls on the top of her head that reminded Theo of a stack of Danish pastries.

The lift reached the second floor and the doors opened.

"Come along, Pixie," she said and she got out.

Theo pushed the button for the ground floor and put on his trainers. One was alarmingly wet.

Theo knocked at Mr Windrush's door.

"Hello, there," said Mr Windrush, opening the

**138**

door. He pushed his spectacles back up his nose. "You'll have come for your post." He handed Theo a stack of letters.

"Thank you, Mr Windrush," said Theo. He saw the top letter was from Russia.

"I see that Cringle's Tower is nearly finished," said Mr Windrush.

"Yes," said Theo. Mr Jellicon had been left with no alternative but to rebuild the tower. Mr and Mrs Jellicon hadn't been seen in Bunting recently. It was rumoured that they were having a long holiday in the Caribbean.

"Better than it was before, I think," said Mr Windrush.

"Yes," agreed Theo.

"Of course, I could have told them that Captain Cringle had left the tower to the town, just by looking at the dust. But nobody asked."

"I expect they didn't think of it," said Theo, feeling slightly guilty.

"Oh well, must get on," said Mr Windrush and he disappeared back inside his room.

Back in the lift, Theo sat on his bed and looked at the letters to see if any were for him. The one from Russia would be the details about his sisters' trip.

There were several brown envelopes for his father, a letter for his mother and one for him. He nearly missed his, it was so pale and thin.

It was difficult to handle, as if it was made of cobwebs. After quite a bit of difficulty Theo succeeded in opening the envelope. There was a card inside with the words:

> *The Bunting Division Hallowe'en Management*
> *Committee*
> *invite*
> *Theo Slugg*
> *to a party at Cringle's Tower*
> *on 31st October at 9 p.m.*
> *RSVP*

Theo wondered how he was supposed to reply.

But was he going? To a Hallowe'en bash for his grandma's friends? Was he barmy?

Theo got a piece of paper and a pen and wrote:

> *Dear Management Committee,*
> *Thank you very much for the invitation.*
> *I'd like to come.*
> *Love Theo*

He folded the bit of paper in two and pressed button B. When the lift reached the basement, he pressed the button again and the lift went on down.

When the lift finally stopped, the doors didn't open. Theo tried pushing the button again but the doors stayed shut. Oh well, thought Theo, and with a shrug he posted his note through the tiny gap between the doors and then pressed the button for the third floor.

When Theo arrived at the tower on Hallowe'en, the ghostly bash was in full swing. There were lots of ghosts, standing around in groups, talking excitedly. Theo clambered up the stairs of the new tower. Amongst the ghosts at the top he found Wat. He had a glass in his hand and waved it when he saw Theo.

"Hello Wat, are you enjoying yourself?" said Theo.

Wat grinned. "Have some gravy?" he asked, holding the glass out to Theo.

"Yuck, no thanks. Don't you drink anything else?"

Wat shook his head.

"Woe! Woe! Woe!" wailed Mrs Cringle. She was wandering up and down, waving her hands in the air.

"What's wrong with her?" said Theo.

"Nothing," said Wat. "She always does that. Oh, Theo, I've been meaning to say. . ."

"Yes?"

"Sorry I fell asleep that night, at Jellicon's house."

"Oh that's all right," said Theo. "I'd forgotten it. Anyway, if it hadn't been for you, that brute might have, you know. . ." Theo tapped Wat affectionately on his shoulder. Wat beamed at him.

Then Theo saw his grandma.

"What are you doing here?" asked Grandma.

"You invited me," said Theo.

"I did not!" said Grandma. "You've got no right to be here. Why, you're not even . . . DEAD!"

"But Grandma, it's all because of me that the party's happening here."

"All because of YOU? You're joking!"

"No I'm not," cried Theo, feeling angry. Why should he put up with this? His grandma never gave him any credit. "You couldn't have done it without me."

"Of course we could!" said Grandma. "We don't need a snivelling snail like you to help us."

"Don't make me laugh, you're all helpless!" cried Theo.

"We're not!" cried Grandma, shooing him away with her stick. "We'll do it on our own, the next time! Go on, go away, you horrid little worm. And don't come back!"

"I won't!" shouted Theo, walking away from her.

Alix was leaning against the wall, feeding her crows through a window. Theo decided not to ask what she was feeding them.

"She didn't mean it," said Alix.

"I don't expect she did," said Theo.

"And she didn't invite you either," said Alix. "Wat and I did."

"You did?"

"Yeah."

For a moment Theo didn't know what to say.

"Thanks Alix," he said finally. Then he remembered something. "Oh, Alix. . . You know when we were here, that time with Drake. . ."

"Yeah, don't worry about it," said Alix. "It's all right. I've forgiven you." She grinned at Theo and he saw she'd painted all her teeth black. "Come on," she said. "The real bash is outside." She waved at Wat to follow and led the way downstairs.

Behind the tower was an open space lit by moonlight. There was a band playing strange tunes and everywhere Theo looked there were ghosts dancing. Theo glimpsed Pete Pilkington tap dancing away in front of a small audience. Pete saw Theo and gave him a cheery wave.

Alix was walking towards the dancing. She paused briefly and turning to Theo said, "You *can* dance, can't you?"